MORGANA

Two Stories from 'The Golden Apples'

Morgana

Two Stories from 'The Golden Apples'

by

Eudora Welty

Illustrated by Mildred Nungester Wolfe

UNIVERSITY PRESS OF MISSISSIPPI

JACKSON AND LONDON

Library of Congress Cataloging in Publication Data

Welty, Eudora, 1909–
    [June recital]
    Morgana: two stories from "The golden apples" / by Eudora Welty:
illustrated by Mildred Nungester Wolfe.
        p.   cm.
    Contents: June recital—Moon Lake.
    ISBN 0-87805-400-6. ISBN 0-87805-401-4 (lim. ed.)
    I. Welty, Eudora, 1909– Moon Lake. 1988. II. Title.
PS3545.E6J86   1988
813'.52—dc19   88-20552
                                                         CIP

CONTENTS

ILLUSTRATIONS

June Recital

vii

ILLUSTRATIONS

Moon Lake

JUNE RECITAL

OCH WAS IN A TEMPEST
with his mother. She would keep him in bed and make him take
Cocoa-Quinine all summer, if she had her way. He yelled and let her
wait holding the brimming spoon, his eyes taking in the whole ironclad
pattern, the checkerboard of her apron—until he gave out of breath,
and took the swallow. His mother laid her hand on his pompadour cap,
wobbled his scalp instead of kissing him, and went off to her nap.

"Louella!" he called faintly, hoping she would come upstairs and he
could devil her into running to Loomis's and buying him an ice cream
cone out of her pocket, but he heard her righteously bang a pot to him
in the kitchen. At last he sighed, stretched his toes—so clean he despised the very sight of his feet—and brought himself up on his elbow
to the window.

Next door was the vacant house.

His family would all be glad if it burned down; he wrapped it with the
summer's love. Beyond the hackberry leaves of their own tree and the
cedar row and the spready yard over there, it stretched its weathered
side. He let his eyes rest or go flickering along it, as over something
very well known indeed. Its left-alone contour, its careless stretching
away into that deep backyard he knew by heart. The house's side was
like a person's, if a person or giant would lie sleeping there, always
sleeping.

A red and bottle-shaped chimney held up all. The roof spread falling to the front, the porch came around the side leaning on the curve, where it hung with bannisters gone, like a cliff in a serial at the Bijou. Instead of cowboys in danger, Miss Jefferson Moody's chickens wandered over there from across the way, flapped over the edge, and found the shade cooler, the dust fluffier to sit in, and the worms thicker under that blackening floor.

In the side of the house were six windows, two upstairs and four down, and back of the chimney a small stair window shaped like a keyhole—one made never to open; they had one like it. There were green shades rolled up to various levels, but not curtains. A table showed in the dining room, but no chairs. The parlor window was in the shadow of the porch and of thin, vibrant bamboo leaves, clear and dark as a pool he knew in the river. There was a piano in the parlor. In addition there were little fancy chairs, like Sunday School chairs or children's drug store chairs, turned this way and that, and the first strong person trying to sit down would break them one after the other. Instead of a door into the hall there was a curtain; it was made of beads. With no air the curtain hung still as a wall and yet you could see through it, if anybody should pass the door.

In that window across from his window, in the back upper room, a bed faced his. The foot was gone, and a mattress had partly slid down but was holding on. A shadow from a tree, a branch and its leaves, slowly traveled over the hills and hollows of the mattress.

In the front room there, the window was dazzling in afternoon; it was raised. Except for one tall post with a hat on it, that bed was out of sight. It was true, there was one person in the house—Loch would recall him sooner or later—but it was only Mr. Holifield. He was the night watchman down at the gin, he always slept all day. A framed picture could be seen hanging on the wall, just askew enough so that it looked straightened every now and then. Sometimes the glass in the picture reflected the light outdoors and the flight of birds between branches of trees, and while it reflected, Mr. Holifield was having a dream.

Loch could look across through cedars that missed one, in the line, and in a sweeping glance see it all—as if he possessed it—from its front porch to its shed-like back and its black-shadowed summerhouse—which was an entirely different love, odorous of black leaves that crumbled into soot; and its shade of four fig trees where he would steal the figs if July ever came. And above all the shade, which was dark as a boat, the blue sky flared—shooting out like a battle, and hot as fire. The hay riders his sister went with at night (went with against their father's will, slipped out by their mother's connivance) would ride off singing, "Oh, It Ain't Gonna Rain No More." Even under his shut eyelids, that light and shade stayed divided from each other, but reversed.

Some whole days at a time, often in his dreams day and night, he would seem to be living next door, wild as a cowboy, absolutely by himself, without his mother or father coming in to feel his skin, or run a finger up under his cap—without one parent to turn on the fan and the other to turn it off, or them both together to pin a newspaper around the light at night to shade him out of their talk. And there was where Cassie could never bring him books to read, miserable girls' books and fairy tales.

It was the leaky gutter over there that woke Loch up, back in the spring when it rained. Splashy as a waterfall in a forest, it shook him with that agony of being *made* to wake up from a sound sleep to be taken away somewhere, made to go. It made his heart beat fast.

They could do what they wanted to to him but they could not take his pompadour cap off him or take his house away. He reached down under the bed and pulled up the telescope.

It was his father's telescope and he was allowed to look through it unmolested as long as he ran a temperature. It was what they gave him instead of his pea-shooter and cap pistol. Smelling of brass and the drawer of the library table where it came from, it was an object hitherto brought out in the family group for eclipses of the moon; and the day the airplane flew over with a lady in it, and they all waited for it all day, wry and aching up at the sky; the telescope had been gripped in his father's hand like a big stick, some kind of protective weapon for what was to come.

Loch fixed the long brass tubes and shot the telescope out the window, propping the screen outward and letting more mosquitoes in, the way he was forbidden. He examined the size of the distant figs: like marbles yesterday, wine-balls today. Getting those would not be the same as stealing. On the other side of fury at confinement a sweet self-indulgence could visit him in his bed. He moved the glass lovingly toward the house and touched its roof, with the little birds on it cocking their heads.

With the telescope to his eye he even smelled the house strongly. Morgana was extra deep in smell this afternoon; the magnolias were open all over the tree at the last corner. They glittered like lights in the dense tree that loomed in the shape of a cave opening at the brought-up-close edge of the Carmichael roof. He looked at the thrush's nest, Woodrow Spights' old ball on the roof, the drift of faded election hand-bills on the porch—the vacant house again, the half of a china plate deep in the weeds; the chickens always went to that plate, and it was dry.

Loch trained the telescope to the back and caught the sailor and the girl in the moment they jumped the ditch. They always came the back way, swinging hands and running low under the leaves. The girl was the piano player at the picture show. Today she was carrying a paper sack from Mr. Wiley Bowles' grocery.

She had let the sailor pick her up and carry her one day, with her fingers lifting to brush the leaves.

Loch squinted; he was waiting for the day when the sailor took the figs. And see what the girl would hurry him into. Her name was Virgie Rainey. She had been in Cassie's room all the way through school, so that made her sixteen; she would ruin any nice idea. She looked like a tomboy but it was not the truth. She had let the sailor pick her up and carry her one day, with her fingers lifting to brush the leaves. It was she that had showed the sailor the house to begin with, she that started him coming. They were rusty old fig trees but the figs were the little sweet blue. When they cracked open, their pink and golden flesh would show, their inside flowers, and golden bubbles of juice would hang, to touch your tongue to first. Loch gave the sailor time, for it was he, Loch, who was in command of leniency here; he was giving him day after day.

He swayed on his knees and saw the sailor and Virgie Rainey in a clear blue-and-white small world run sparkling to the back door of the empty house.

And next would come the old man going by in the blue wagon, up as far as the Starks' and back to the Carmichaels' corner.

> *"Buttermilk?*
> *Buttermilk.*
> *Fresh dewberries and—*
> *Buttermilk."*

That was Mr. Fate Rainey and his song. He would take a long time to pass. Loch could study through the telescope the new flower in his horse's hat each day. He would go past the Starks' and circle the cemetery and niggertown, and come back again. His cry, with a song's tune, would come near, then far, and near again. Was it an echo—was an echo that? Or was it, for the last time, the call of somebody seeking about in a deep cave, "Here—here! Oh, here am I!"

There was a sound that might have been a blue jay scolding, and that was the back door; they were just now going in off the back porch.

8

When he saw the door prized open—the stretched screen billowing from being too freely leaned against—and let the people in, Loch felt the old indignation rise up. But at the same time he felt joy. For while the invaders did not see him, he saw them, both with the naked eye and through the telescope; and each day that he kept them to himself, they were his.

Louella appeared below on their steps and with a splash threw out the dirty dishwater in the direction of the empty house. But she would never speak, and he would never speak. He had not shared anybody in his life even with Louella.

After the door fell at the sailor's heel, and the upstairs window had been forced up and propped, then silence closed over the house next door. It closed over just as silence did in their house at this time of day; but like the noisy waterfall it kept him awake—fighting sleep.

In the beginning, before he saw anyone, he would just as soon have lain there and thought of wild men holding his house in thrall, or of a giant crouched double behind the window that corresponded to his own. The big fig tree was many times a magic tree with golden fruit that shone in and among its branches like a cloud of lightning bugs—a tree twinkling all over, burning, on and off, off and on. The sweet golden juice to come—in his dream he put his tongue out, and then his mother would be putting that spoon in his mouth.

More than once he dreamed it was inside that house that the cave had moved, and the buttermilk man went in and out the rooms driving his horse with its red rose and berating its side with a whip that unfurled of itself; in the dream he was not singing. Or the horse itself, a white and beautiful one, was on its way over, approaching to ask some favor of him, a request called softly and intelligibly upward—which he was not decided yet whether to grant or deny. This call through the window had not yet happened—not quite. But someone had come.

He turned away. "Cassie!" he cried.

9

Cassie came to his room. She said, "Didn't I tell you what you could do? Trim up those Octagon Soap coupons and count them good if you want that jack-knife." Then she went off again and slammed her door. He seemed to see her belatedly. She had been dressed up for whatever she was doing in her room like somebody in the circus, with colored spots on her, and hardly looked like his sister.

"You looked silly when you came in!" he called.

But over at the empty house was a stillness not of going off and leaving him but of coming nearer. Something was coming very close to him, there was something he had better keep track of. He had the feeling that something was being counted. Then he too must count. He could be wary enough that way, counting by ones, counting by fives, by tens. Sometimes he threw his arm across his eyes and counted without moving his lips, imagining that when he got to a certain amount he might give a yell, like "Coming, ready or not!" and go down by the hackberry limb. He never had yelled, and his arm was a heavy weight across his face. Often that was the way he fell asleep. He woke up drenched with the afternoon fever breaking. Then his mother pulled him and pushed him as she put cool pillow cases on the pillows and pushed him back straight. She was doing it now.

"Now your powder."

His mother, dressed up for a party, tilted the little pinked paper toward his stuck-out, protesting tongue, and guided the glass of water into his groping hand. Every time he got a powder swallowed, she said calmly, "Dr. Loomis only gives you these to satisfy me you're getting medication." His father, when he came home from the office, would say, "Well, if you've got malaria, son . . ." (kissing him) ". . . you've got malaria, that's all there is to it. Ha! Ha! Ha!"

"I've made you some junket, too," she said with a straight face.

He made a noise calculated to sicken her, and she smiled at him.

10

"When I come back from Miss Nell Carlisle's I'll bring you all the news of Morgana."

He could not help but smile at her—lips shut. She was almost his ally. She swung her little reticule at him and went off to the Rook party. By leaning far out he could see a lackadaisical, fluttery kind of parade, the ladies of Morgana under their parasols, all trying to keep cool while they walked down to Miss Nell's. His mother was absorbed into their floating, transparent colors. Miss Perdita Mayo was talking, and they were clicking their summery heels and drowning out—drowning out something. . . .

A little tune was playing on the air, and it was coming from the piano in the vacant house.

The tune came again, like a touch from a small hand that he had unwittingly pushed away. Loch lay back and let it persist. All at once tears rolled out of his eyes. He opened his mouth in astonishment. Then the little tune seemed the only thing in the whole day, the whole summer, the whole season of his fevers and chills, that was accountable: it was personal. But he could not tell why it was so.

It came like a signal, or a greeting—the kind of thing a horn would play out in the woods. He halfway closed his eyes. It came and trailed off and was lost in the neighborhood air. He heard it and then wondered how it went.

It took him back to when his sister was so sweet, to a long time ago. To when they loved each other in a different world, a boundless, trustful country all its own, where no mother or father came, either through sweetness or impatience—different altogether from his solitary world now, where he looked out all eyes like Argus, on guard everywhere.

A spoon went against a dish, three times. In her own room Cassie was carrying on some girls' business that, at least, smelled terrible to

11

him, as bad as when she painted a hair-receiver with rosebuds and caught it on fire drying it. He heard Louella talking to herself in the lower hall. "Louella!" he called, flat on his back, and she called up for him to favor her with some rest or she would give up the ghost right then. When he drew up to the window again, the first thing he saw was someone new, coming along the walk out front.

Here came an old lady. No, she was an old woman, round and unsteady-looking—unsteady the way he felt himself when he got out of bed—not on her way to a party. She must have walked in from out in the country. He saw her stop in front of the vacant house, turn herself, and go up the front walk.

Something besides countriness gave her her look. Maybe it came from her having nothing in her hands, no reticule or fan. She looked as if she could even be the one who lived in the house and had just stepped outside for a moment to see if it was going to rain and now, matter-of-factly, a little toilsomely with so much to do, was going back in.

But when she began to hasten, Loch got the idea she might be the sailor's mother come after her son. The sailor didn't belong in Morgana anyhow. Whoever she was, she climbed the steps and crossed the wobbly porch and put her hand to the front door, which she opened just as easily as Virgie Rainey had opened the back door. She went inside, and he saw her through the beady curtain, which made her outline quiver for a moment.

Suppose doors with locks and keys were ever locked—then nothing like this would have the chance to happen. The nearness of missing things, and the possibility of preventing them, made Loch narrow his eyes.

Three party ladies who were late and puffing, all hurrying together in a duck-like line, now passed. They just missed sight of the old woman— Miss Jefferson Moody, Miss Mamie Carmichael, and Miss Billy Texas

12

Spights. They would have stopped everything. Then in the middle of the empty air behind everybody, butterflies suddenly crossed and circled each other, their wings digging and flashing like duelers' swords in the vacuum.

Though Loch was gratified with the outrage mounting—three people now were in the vacant house—and could consider whether the old woman might have come to rout out the other two and give them her tirade, he was puzzled when the chandelier lighted up in the parlor. He ran the telescope out the window again and put his frowning eye to it. He discovered the old woman moving from point to point all around the parlor, in and out of the little chairs, sidling along the piano. He could not see her feet; she behaved a little like a wind-up toy on wheels, rolling into the corners and edges of objects and being diverted and sent on, but never out of the parlor.

He moved his eye upstairs, up an inch on the telescope. There on a mattress delightfully bare—where he would love, himself, to lie, on a slant and naked, to let the little cottony tufts annoy him and to feel the mattress like billows bouncing beneath, and to eat pickles lying on his back—the sailor and the piano player lay and ate pickles out of an open sack between them. Because of the down-tilt of the mattress, the girl had to keep watch on the sack, and when it began to slide down out of reach that was when they laughed. Sometimes they held pickles stuck in their mouths like cigars, and turned to look at each other. Sometimes they lay just alike, their legs in an M and their hands joined between them, exactly like the paper dolls his sister used to cut out of folded newspaper and unfold to let him see. If Cassie would come in now, he would point out the window and she would remember.

And then, like the paper dolls sprung back together, they folded close—the real people. Like a big grasshopper lighting, all their legs and arms drew in to one small body, deadlike, with protective coloring.

13

He leaned back and bent his head against the cool side of the pillow and shut his eyes, and felt tired out. He clasped the cool telescope to his side, and with his fingernail closed its little eye.

"Poor old Telescope," he said.

When he looked out again, everybody next door was busier.

Upstairs, the sailor and Virgie Rainey were running in circles around the room, each time jumping with outstretched arms over the broken bed. Who chased whom had nothing to do with it because they kept the same distance between them. They went around and around like the policeman and Charlie Chaplin, both intending to fall down.

Downstairs, the sailor's mother was doing something just as fanciful. She was putting up decorations. (Cassie would be happy to see that.) As if she were giving a party that day, she was dressing up the parlor with ribbons of white stuff. It was newspaper.

The old woman left the parlor time and time again and reappeared— in and out through the beads in the doorway—each time with an armful of old *Bugles* that had lain on the back porch in people's way for a long time. And from her gestures of eating crumbs or pulling bits of fluff from her bosom, Loch recognized that mother-habit: she had pins there. She pinned long strips of the newspaper together, first tearing them carefully and evenly as a school teacher. She made ribbons of newspaper and was hanging them all over the parlor, starting with the piano, where she weighted down the ends with a statue.

When Loch grew tired of watching one animated room he watched the other. How the two playing would whirl and jump over the old woman's head! That was the way the bed fell to begin with.

As Loch leaned his chin in his palm at the window and watched, it seemed strangely as if he had seen this whole thing before. The old woman was decorating the piano until it rayed out like a Christmas tree or a Maypole. Maypole ribbons of newspaper and tissue paper streamed

14

Loch then leapt to his knees, crawled out the window under the pushed-out screen, onto the hackberry branch, and let himself into the tree the old way.

and crossed each other from the piano to the chandelier and festooned again to the four corners of the room, looped to the backs of chairs here and there. When would things begin?

Soon everything seemed fanciful and beautiful enough to Loch; he thought she could stop. But the old woman kept on. This was only a part of something in her head. And in the splendor she fixed and pinned together she was all alone. She was not connected with anything else, with anybody. She was one old woman in a house not bent on dealing punishment. Though once when Woody Spights and his sister came by on skates, of course she came out and ran them away.

Once she left the house, to come right back. With her unsteady but purposeful walk, as if she were on a wheel that misguided her, she crossed the road to the Carmichael yard and came back with some green leaves and one bloom from the magnolia tree—carried in her skirt. She pulled the corners of her skirt up like a girl, and she was thin beneath in her old legs. But she zigzagged across the road—such a show-off, carefree way for a mother to behave, but mothers sometimes did. She lifted her elbows—as if she might skip! But nobody saw her: his forehead was damp. He heard a scream from the Rook party up at Miss Nell's—it sounded like Miss Jefferson Moody shooting-the-moon. Nobody saw the old woman but Loch, and he told nothing.

She brought the bunch of green into the parlor and put it on the piano, where the Maypole crown would go. Then she took a step back and was as admiring as if somebody else had done it—nodding her head.

But after she had the room all decorated to suit her, she kept on, and began to stuff the cracks. She brought in more paper and put it in all the cracks at the windows. Now Loch realized that the windows in the parlor were both down, it was tight as a box, and she had been inside in the suffocating heat. A wave of hotness passed over his body. Furthermore, she made her way with a load of *Bugles* to the blind part of the

16

wall where he knew the fireplace was. All the load went into the fireplace.

When she went out of the parlor again she came back slowly indeed. She was pushing a big square of matting along on its side; she wove and bent and struggled behind it, like a spider with something bigger than he can eat, pushing it into the parlor. Loch was suddenly short of breath and pressed forward, cramped inside, checkerboarding his forehead and nose against the screen. He both wanted the plot to work and wanted it to fail. In another moment he was shed of all the outrage and the possessiveness he had felt for the vacant house. This house was something the old woman intended to burn down. And Loch could think of a thousand ways she could do it better.

She could fetch a mattress—that would burn fine. Suppose she went upstairs now for the one they played on? Or pulled the other one, sheet and all, from under Mr. Holifield (whose hat had imperceptibly turned on the bedpost; it changed like a weathercock)? If she went out of sight for a minute, he watched at the little stair window, but she did not go up.

She brought in an old quilt that the dogs there once slept on, that had hung over the line on the back porch until it was half light-colored and half dark. She climbed up on the piano stool, the way women climb, death-defying, and hung the quilt over the front window. It fell down. Twice more she climbed up with it and the third time it stayed. If only she did not block the window toward him! But if she meant to, she forgot. She kept putting her hand to her head.

Everything she did was wrong, after a certain point. She had got off the track. What she really wanted was a draft. Instead, she was keeping air away, and let her try to make fire burn in an airless room. That was the conceited thing girls and women would try.

But now she went to the blind corner of the parlor and when she came out she had a new and mysterious object in her hands.

At that moment Loch heard Louella climbing the back stairs, coming to peep in at him. He flung himself on his back, stretched out one arm, his hand on his heart and his mouth agape, as he did when he played dead in battle. He forgot to shut his eyes. Louella stood there a minute and then tiptoed off.

Loch then leapt to his knees, crawled out the window under the pushed-out screen, onto the hackberry branch, and let himself into the tree the old way.

He went out on a far-extending limb that took him nearest the vacant house. With him at their window the sailor and girl saw him and yet did not see him. He descended further. He found his place in the tree, a rustling, familiar old crotch where he used to sit and count up his bottle tops. He hung watching, sometimes by the hands and sometimes by the knees and feet.

The old woman was dirty. Standing still she shook a little—her hanging cheeks and her hands. He could see well now what she was holding there like a lamp. But he could not tell what it was—a small brown wooden box, shaped like the Obelisk. It had a door—she opened it. It made a mechanical sound. He heard it plainly through the boxed room which was like a sounding board; it was ticking.

She set the obelisk up on the piano, there in the crown of leaves; she pushed a statue out of the way. He listened to it ticking on and his hopes suddenly rose for her. Holding by the knees and diving head down, then swaying in the sweet open free air and dizzy as an apple on a tree, he thought: the box is where she has the dynamite.

He opened his arms and let them hang outward, and flickered his lashes in the June light, watching house, sky, leaves, a flying bird, all and nothing at all.

Little Sister Spights, aged two, that he had not seen cross the street since she was born, wandered under him dragging a skate.

"Hello, little bitty old sweet thing," he murmured from the leaves. "Better go back where you came from."

18

He hung watching, sometimes by the hands and sometimes by the knees and feet.

And then the old woman stuck out a finger and played the tune.
He hung still as a folded bat.

II

Für Elise.

In her bedroom when she heard the gentle opening, the little phrase,
Cassie looked up from what she was doing and said in response, "Virgie Rainey, *danke schoen.*"

In surprise, but as slowly as in regret, she stopped stirring the emerald green. She got up from where she had been squatting in the middle
of the floor and stepped over the dishes which were set about on the
matting rug. She went quietly to her south window, where she lifted a
curtain, spotting it with her wet fingers. There was not a soul in sight at
the MacLain house but Old Man Holifield asleep with his gawky high-
top shoes on and his stomach full as a robin's. His presence—he was
the Holifield who was night watchman at the gin and slept here by
day—never kept Cassie's mother from going right ahead and calling
the MacLain house "the vacant house."

Whatever you called it, the house was something you saw without
seeing it—it was part of the world again. That unpainted side changed
passively with the day and the season, the way a natural place like the
river bank changed. In cooler weather its windows would turn like
sweetgum leaves, maroon when the late sun came up, and in winter it
was bare and glinty, more exposed and more lonesome even than now.
In summer it was an overgrown place. Leaves and their shadows pressed
up to it, arc-light sharp and still as noon all day. It showed at all times
that no woman kept it.

That rainless, windless June the bright air and the town of Morgana,
life itself, sunlit and moonlit, were composed and still and china-like.
Cassie felt that now. Yet in the shade of the vacant house, though all
looked still, there was agitation. Some life stirred through. It may have
been *old* life.

20

Ever since the MacLains had moved away, that roof had stood (and leaked) over the heads of people who did not really stay, and a restless current seemed to flow dark and free around it (there would be some sound or motion to startle the birds), a life quicker than the Morrisons' life, more driven probably, thought Cassie uneasily.

Was it Virgie Rainey in there now? Where was she hiding, if she sneaked in and touched that piano? When did she come? Cassie felt teased. She doubted for a moment that she had heard *Für Elise*—she doubted herself, so easily, and she struck her chest with her fist, sighing, the way Parnell Moody always struck hers.

A line of poetry tumbled in her ears, or started to tumble.

"Though I am old with wandering . . ."

She banged her hands on her hipbones, enough to hurt, flung around, and went back to her own business. On one bare foot with the other crossed over it, she stood gazing down at the pots and dishes in which she had enough colors stirred up to make a sunburst design. She was shut up in here to tie-and-dye a scarf. "Everybody stay out!!!" said an envelope pinned to her door, signed with skull and crossbones.

You took a square of crepe de Chine, you made a point of the goods and tied a string around it in hard knots. You kept on gathering it in and tying it. Then you hung it in the different dyes. The strings were supposed to leave white lines in the colors, a design like a spiderweb. You couldn't possibly have any idea what you would get when you untied your scarf; but Missie Spights said there had never been one yet that didn't take the breath away.

Für Elise. This time there were two phrases, the *E* in the second phrase very flat.

Cassie edged back to the window, while her heart sank, praying that she would not catch sight of Virgie Rainey or, especially, that Virgie Rainey would not catch sight of her.

Virgie Rainey worked. Not at teaching. She played the piano for the picture show, both shows every night, and got six dollars a week, and

There she was now, standing scared at the window again
in her petticoat.

was not popular any more. Even in her last year in consolidated high school—just ended—she worked. But when Cassie and she were little, they used to take music together in the MacLain house next door, from Miss Eckhart. Virgie Rainey played *Für Elise* all the time. And Miss Eckhart used to say, "Virgie Rainey, *danke schoen.*" Where had Miss Eckhart ever gone? She had been Miss Snowdie MacLain's roomer.

"Cassie!" Loch was calling again.

"What!"

"Come here!"

"I can't!"

"Got something to show you!"

"I *ain't got time!*"

Her bedroom door had been closed all afternoon. But first her mother had opened it and come in, only to exclaim and not let herself be touched, and to go out leaving the smell of rose geranium behind for the fan to keep bringing at her. Then Louella had moved right in on her without asking and for ages was standing over her rolling up her hair on newspaper to make it bushy for the hayride that night. "I cares if you don't."

With her gaze at a judicious distance from the colors she dipped in, Cassie was now for a little time far away, perhaps up in September in college, where, however, tie-and-dye scarves would be out-of-uniform, though something to unfold and show.

But with *Für Elise* the third time, her uncritical self of the crucial present, this Wednesday afternoon, slowly came forward—as if called on. Cassie saw herself without even facing the mirror, for her small, solemn, unprotected figure was emerging staring-clear inside her mind. There she was now, standing scared at the window again in her petticoat, a little of each color of the rainbow dropped on her—bodice and flounce—in spite of reasonable care. Her pale hair was covered and burdened with twisty papers, like a hat too big for her. She balanced her head on her frail neck. She was holding a spoon up like a mean switch in her right hand, and her feet were bare. She had seemed to be favored and happy and she stood there pathetic—homeless-looking—horrible. Like a wave, the gathering past came right up to her. Next time it would be too high. The poetry was all around her, pellucid and lifting from side to side,

> *"Though I am old with wandering*
> *Through hollow lands and hilly lands,*
> *I will find out where she has gone. . . ."*

Then the wave moved up, towered, and came drowning down over her stuck-up head.

Through the years Cassie had come just before Virgie Rainey for her music lesson, or, at intervals, just after her. To start with, Cassie was so poor in music and Virgie so good (the opposite of themselves in other things!) that Miss Eckhart with her methodical mind might have coupled them on purpose. They went on Mondays and Thursdays at 3:30 and 4:00 and, after school was out and up until the recital, at 9:30 and 10:00 in the morning. So punctual and so formidable was Miss Eckhart that all the little girls passed, one going and one coming, through the beaded curtains mincing like strangers. Only Virgie would let go the lights of mockery from her eyes.

Though she was tireless as a spider, Miss Eckhart waited so unbudgingly for her pupils that from the back she appeared asleep in her studio. How much later had it occurred to Cassie that "the studio" itself, the only one ever heard of in Morgana, was nothing more than a room that was rented? Rented because poor Miss Snowdie MacLain needed the money?

Then it seemed a dedicated place. The black-painted floor was bare even of matting, so as not to deaden any sound of music. There was in the very center a dark squarish piano (ebony, they all thought) with legs twisted like elephant legs, bearing many pounds of sheet music on its back—just to look heavy there, Cassie thought, for whose music was it? The yellow keys, some split and others in the bass coffee-colored, always had a little film of sweat. There was a stool spun up high, with a seat worn away like a bowl. Beside it, Miss Eckhart's chair was the kind of old thing most people placed by their telephones.

There were gold chairs, their legs brittle and set the way pulled candy was, sliding across the floor at a touch, and forbidden—they were for the recital audience; their fragility was intentional. There were taboret tables with little pink statuettes and hydrangea-colored, horny shells. Beaded curtains in the doorway stirred and clicked now and then during a lesson, as if someone were coming, but it signified no more than the idle clicking redbirds made in the free outdoors, if it was not time for a pupil. (The MacLains lived largely upstairs, except for the kitchen, and came in at the side.) The beads were faintly sweet-smelling, and made you think of long strings of wine-balls and tiny candy bottles filled with violet liquid, and licorice sticks. The studio was in some ways like the witch's house in *Hansel and Gretel*, Cassie's mother said, "including the witch." On the right-hand corner of the piano stood a small, mint-white bust of Beethoven, all softened around the edges with the nose smoothed down, as if a cow had licked it.

Miss Eckhart, a heavy brunette woman whose age was not known, sat during the lessons on the nondescript chair, which her body hid altogether, in apparent disregard for body and chair alike. She was alternately very quiet and very alert, and sometimes that seemed to be because she hated flies. She held a swatter in her down-inclined lap, gracefully and tenderly as a fan, her hard, round, short fingers surprisingly forgetful-looking. All at once as you played your piece, making errors or going perfectly it did not matter, smack down would come the fly swatter on the back of your hand. No words would be passed, of triumph or apology on Miss Eckhart's part or of surprise or pain on yours. It did hurt. Virgie, her face hardening under the progress of her advancing piece, could manage the most oblivious look of all, though Miss Eckhart might strike harder and harder at the persistent flies. All her pupils let the flies in, when they trailed in and out for their lessons; not to speak of the MacLain boys, who left their door wide open to the universe when they went out to play.

Miss Eckhart might also go abruptly to her little built-on kitchen— she and her mother had no Negro and didn't use Miss Snowdie's; she did not say "Excuse me," or explain what was on the stove. And there were times, perhaps on rainy days, when she walked around and around the studio, and you felt her pause behind you. Just as you thought she had forgotten you, she would lean over your head, you were under her bosom like a traveler under a cliff, her penciled finger would go to your music, and above the bar you were playing she would slowly write "Slow." Or sometimes, precipitant above you, she would make a curly circle with a long tail, as if she might draw a cat, but it would be her "P" and the word would turn into "Practice!!"

When you could once play a piece, she paid scant attention, and made no remark; her manners were all very unfamiliar. It was only time for a new piece. Whenever she opened the cabinet, the smell of new sheet music came out swift as an imprisoned spirit, something almost palpable, like a pet coon; Miss Eckhart kept the music locked up and the key down her dress, inside the collar. She would seat herself and with a dipped pen add "$.25" to the bill on the spot. Cassie could see the bills clearly, in elaborate handwriting, the "z" in Mozart with an equals-sign through it and all the "y's" so heavily tailed they went through the paper. It took a whole lesson for those tails to dry.

What was it she did when you played without a mistake? Oh, she went over and told the canary something, tapping the bars of his cage with her finger. "Just listen," she told him. "Enough from *you* for to-day," she would call to you over her shoulder.

Virgie Rainey would come through the beads carrying a magnolia bloom which she had stolen.

She would ride over on a boy's bicycle (her brother Victor's) from the Raineys' with sheets of advanced music rolled naked (girls usually had portfolios) and strapped to the boy's bar which she straddled, the magnolia broken out of the Carmichaels' tree and laid bruising in the wire basket on the handlebars. Or sometimes Virgie would come an hour late, if she had to deliver the milk first, and sometimes she came by the back door and walked in peeling a ripe fig with her teeth; and sometimes she missed her lesson altogether. But whenever she came on the bicycle she would ride it up into the yard and run the front wheel bang into the lattice, while Cassie was playing the "Scarf Dance." (In those days, the house looked nice, with latticework and plants hiding the foundation, and a three-legged fern stand at the turn in the porch to discourage skaters and defeat little boys.) Miss Eckhart would put her hand to her breast, as though she felt the careless wheel shake the very foundation of the studio.

Virgie carried in the magnolia bloom like a hot tureen, and offered it to Miss Eckhart, neither of them knowing any better: magnolias smelled too sweet and heavy for right after breakfast. And Virgie handled everything with her finger stuck out; she was conceited over a musician's cyst that appeared on her fourth finger.

Miss Eckhart took the flower but Virgie might be kept waiting while Cassie recited on her catechism page. Sometimes Miss Eckhart checked the questions missed, sometimes the questions answered; but every question she did check got a heavy "V" that crossed the small page like the tail of a comet. She would draw her black brows together to see Cassie forgetting, unless it was to remember some nearly forgotten thing herself. At the exact moment of the hour (the alarm clock had a green and blue waterfall scene on its face) she would dismiss Cassie and incline her head toward Virgie, as though she was recognizing her

27

And when she finished, Miss Eckhart would say,
"Virgie Rainey, danke schoen."

only now, when she was ready for her; yet all this time she had held the strong magnolia flower in her hand, and its scent was filling the room.

Virgie would drift over to the piano, spread out her music, and make sure she was sitting just the way she wanted to be upon the stool. She flung her skirt behind her, with a double swimming motion. Then without a word from Miss Eckhart she would start to play. She played firmly, smoothly, her face at rest, the musician's cyst, of which she was in idleness so proud, perched like a ladybug, riding the song. She went now gently, now forcibly, never loudly.

And when she was finished, Miss Eckhart would say, "Virgie Rainey, *danke schoen.*"

Cassie, so still her chest cramped, not daring to walk on the creaky floor down the hall, would wait till the end to run out of the house and home. She would whisper while she ran, with the sound of an engine, *"Danke schoen, danke schoen, danke schoen."* It wasn't the meaning that propelled her; she didn't know then what it meant.

But then nobody knew for years (until the World War) what Miss Eckhart meant by *"Danke schoen"* and *"Mein lieber Kind"* and the rest, and who would dare ask? It was like belling the cat. Only Virgie had the nerve, only she could have found out for the others. Virgie said she did not know and did not care. So they just added that onto Virgie's name in the school yard. She was Virgie Rainey *Danke schoen* when she jumped hot pepper or fought the boys, when she had to sit down the very first one in the spelling match for saying "E-a-r, ear, r-a-k-e, rake, ear-ache." She was named for good. Sometimes even in the Bijou somebody cat-called that to her as she came in her high heels down the steep slant of the board aisle to switch on the light and open the piano. When she was grown she would tilt up her chin. Calm as a marble head, defamed with a spit-curl, Virgie's head would be proudly carried past the banner on the wall, past every word of "It's Cool at the Bijou, Enjoy Typhoons of Alaskan Breezes," which was tacked up under the fan. Rats ran under her feet, most likely, too; the Bijou was once Spights' Livery Stable.

"Virgie brings me good luck!" Miss Eckhart used to say, with a round smile on her face. Luck that might not be good was something else that was a new thought to them all.

Virgie Rainey, when she was ten or twelve, had naturally curly hair, silky and dark, and a great deal of it—uncombed. She was not sent to the barber shop often enough to suit the mothers of other children, who said it was probably dirty hair too—what could the children see of the back of her neck, poor Katie Rainey being so rushed for time? Her middy blouse was trimmed in a becoming red, her anchor was always loose, and her red silk lacers were actually ladies' shoestrings dipped in pokeberry juice. She was full of the airs of wildness, she swayed and gave way to joys and tempers, her own and other people's with equal freedom—except never Miss Eckhart's, of course.

School did not lessen Virgie's vitality; once on a rainy day when recess was held in the basement, she said she was going to butt her brains out against the wall, and the teacher, old Mrs. McGillicuddy, had said, "Beat them out, then," and she had really tried. The rest of the fourth grade stood around expectant and admiring, the smell of open thermos bottles sweetly heavy in the close air. Virgie came with strange kinds of sandwiches—everybody wanted to swap her—stewed peach, or perhaps banana. In the other children's eyes she was as exciting as a gypsy would be.

Virgie's air of abandon that was so strangely endearing made even the Sunday School class think of her in terms of the future—she would go somewhere, somewhere away off, they said then, talking with their chins sunk in their hands—she'd be a missionary. (Parnell Moody used to be wild and now *she* was pious.) Miss Lizzie Stark's mother, old Mrs. Sad-Talking Morgan, said Virgie would be the first lady governor of Mississippi, that was where she would go. It sounded worse than the infernal regions. To Cassie, Virgie was a secret love, as well as her secret hate. To Cassie she looked like an illustration by Reginald Birch for a serial in Etta Carmichael's *St. Nicholas Magazine* called "The Lucky Stone." Her inky hair fell in the same loose locks—because it was dirty. She often took the very pose of that inventive and persecuted little heroine who coped with people she thought were witches and ogres (alas! they were not)—feet apart, head aslant, eyes glancing up sideways, ears cocked; but you could not tell whether Virgie would boldly interrupt her enemies or run off to her own devices with a forgetful smile on her lips.

And she smelled of flavoring. She drank vanilla out of the bottle, she told them, and it didn't burn her a bit. She did that because she knew they called her mother Miss Ice Cream Rainey, for selling cones at speakings.

Für Elise was always Virgie Rainey's piece. For years Cassie thought Virgie wrote it, and Virgie never did deny it. It was a kind of signal that Virgie had burst in; she would strike that little opening phrase off the keys as she passed anybody's piano—even the one in the café. She never abandoned *Für Elise*; long after she went on to the hard pieces, she still played that.

Virgie Rainey was gifted. Everybody said that could not be denied. To show her it was not denied, she was allowed to play all through school for the other children to march in and to play for Wand Drill. Sometimes they drilled to "Dorothy, an Old English Dance," and sometimes to *Für Elise*—everybody out of kilter.

"I guess they scraped up the money for music lessons somehow," said Cassie's mother. Cassie, when she heard Virgie running her scales next door, would see a vision of the Rainey dining room—an interior which in life she had never seen, for she didn't go home from school with the Raineys—and sitting around the table Miss Katie Rainey and

Cassie, out of nice feeling, looked the other way when it was time for the morning opening of the safe.

Old Man Fate Rainey and Berry and Bolivar Mayhew, some cousins, and Victor who was going to be killed in the war, and Virgie waiting; with Miss Katie scraping up nickels and pennies with an old bone-handled knife, patting them into shape like her butter, and each time— as the scale went up—just barely getting enough or—as it went down— not quite.

Cassie was Miss Eckhart's first pupil, the reason she "took" being that she lived right next door, but she never had any glory from it. When Virgie began "taking," she was the one who made things evident about Miss Eckhart, her lessons, and all. Miss Eckhart, for all her being so strict and inexorable, in spite of her walk, with no give what-soever, had a timid spot in her soul. There was a little weak place in her, vulnerable, and Virgie Rainey found it and showed it to people.

Miss Eckhart worshiped her metronome. She kept it, like the most precious secret in the teaching of music, in a wall safe. Jinny Love Stark, who was only seven or eight years old but had her tongue, did suggest that this was the only thing Miss Eckhart owned of the correct size to lock up there. Why there had ever been a real safe built into the parlor nobody seemed to know; Cassie remembered Miss Snowdie say-ing the Lord knew, in His infinite workings and wisdom, and some day, somebody would come riding in to Morgana and have need of that safe, after she was gone.

Its door looked like a tin plate there in the wall, the closed-up end of an old flue. Miss Eckhart would go toward it with measured step. Tech-nically the safe was hidden, of course, and only she knew it was there, since Miss Snowdie rented it; even Miss Eckhart's mother, possibly, had no expectations of getting in. Yes, her mother lived with her.

Cassie, out of nice feeling, looked the other way when it was time for the morning opening of the safe. It seemed awful, and yet imminent, that because she was the first pupil she, Cassie Morrison, might be the one to call logical attention to the absurdity of a safe in which there were no jewels, in which there was the very opposite of a jewel. Then Virgie, one day when the metronome was set going in front of her—Cassie was just leaving—announced simply that she would not play another note with that thing in her face.

At Virgie's words, Miss Eckhart quickly—it almost seemed that was what she'd wanted to hear—stopped the hand and slammed the little door, bang. The metronome was never set before Virgie again.

Of course all the rest of them still got it. It came out of the safe every morning, as regularly as the canary was uncovered in his cage. Miss Eckhart had made an exception of Virgie Rainey; she had first respected Virgie Rainey, and now fell humble before her impudence.

A metronome was an infernal machine, Cassie's mother said when Cassie told on Virgie. "Mercy, you have to keep moving, with that infernal machine. I want a song to *dip*."

"What do you mean, dip? Could you have played the piano, Mama?"

"Child, I could have *sung*," and she threw her hand from her, as though all music might as well now go jump off the bridge.

As time went on, Virgie Rainey showed her bad manners to Miss Eckhart still more, since she had won about the metronome. Once she had a little *Rondo* her way, and Miss Eckhart was so beset about it that the lesson was not like a real lesson at all. Once she unrolled the new *Étude* and when it kept rolling back up, as the *Étude* always did, she threw it on the floor and jumped on it, before Miss Eckhart had even seen it; that was heartless. After such showing off, Virgie would push her hair behind her ears and then softly lay her hands on the keys, as she would take up a doll.

Miss Eckhart would sit there blotting out her chair in the same way as ever, but inside her she was listening to every note. Such listening would have made Cassie forget. And half the time, the piece was only

Für Elise, which Miss Eckhart could probably have played blindfolded and standing up with her back to the keys. Anybody could tell that Virgie was doing something to Miss Eckhart. She was turning her from a teacher into something lesser. And if she was not a teacher, what was Miss Eckhart?

At times she could not bring herself to swat a summer fly. And as little as Virgie, of them all, cared if her hand was rapped, Miss Eckhart would raise her swatter and try to bring it down and could not. You could see torment in her regard of the fly. The smooth clear music would move on like water, beautiful and undisturbed, under the hanging swatter and Miss Eckhart's red-rimmed thumb. But even boys hit Virgie, because she liked to fight.

There were times when Miss Eckhart's Yankeeness, if not her very origin, some last quality to fade, almost faded. Before some caprice of Virgie's, her spirit drooped its head. The child had it by the lead. Cassie saw Miss Eckhart's spirit as a terrifyingly gentle water-buffalo cow in the story of "Peasie and Beansie" in the reader. And sooner or later, after taming her teacher, Virgie was going to mistreat her. Most of them expected some great scene.

There was in the house itself, soon, a daily occurrence to distress Miss Eckhart. There was now a second roomer at Miss Snowdie's. While Miss Eckhart listened to a pupil, Mr. Voight would walk over their heads and come down to the turn of the stairs, open his bathrobe, and flap the skirts like an old turkey gobbler. They all knew Miss Snowdie never suspected she housed a man like that: he was a sewing machine salesman. When he flapped his maroon-colored bathrobe, he wore no clothes at all underneath.

It would be plain to Miss Eckhart or to anybody that he wanted, first, the music lesson to stop. They could not close the door, there was no door, there were beads. They could not tell Miss Snowdie even that he objected; she would have been agonized. All the little girls and the one

35

little boy were afraid of Mr. Voight's appearance at every lesson and felt nervous until it had happened and got over with. The one little boy was Scooter MacLain, the twin that took the free lessons; he kept mum.

Cassie saw that Miss Eckhart, who might once have been formidable in particular to any Mr. Voights, was helpless toward him and his antics—as helpless as Miss Snowdie MacLain would have been, helpless as Miss Snowdie was, toward her own little twin sons—all since she had begun giving in to Virgie Rainey. Virgie kept the upper hand over Miss Eckhart even at the moment when Mr. Voight came out to scare them. She only played on the stronger and clearer, and never pretended he had not come out and that she did not know it, or that she might not tell it, no matter how poor Miss Eckhart begged.

"Tell a soul what you have seen, I'll beat your hands until you scream," Miss Eckhart had said. Her round eyes opened wide, her mouth went small. This was all she knew to say. To Cassie it was as idle as a magic warning in a story; she criticized the rhyme. She herself had told all about Mr. Voight at breakfast, stood up at the table and waved her arms, only to have her father say he didn't believe it; that Mr. Voight represented a large concern and covered seven states. He added his own threat to Miss Eckhart's: no picture show money.

Her mother's laugh, which followed, was as usual soft and playful but not illuminating. Her laugh, like the morning light that came in the window each summer breakfast time around her father's long head, slowly made it its solid silhouette where he sat against the day. He turned to his paper like Douglas Fairbanks opening big gates; it was indeed his; he published the *Morgana-MacLain Weekly Bugle* and Mr. Voight had no place in it.

"Live and let live, Cassie," her mother said, meaning it mischievously. She showed no repentance, such as Cassie felt, for her inconsistencies. She had sometimes said passionately, "Oh, I hate that old MacLain house next door to me! I hate having it there all the time. I'm

36

worn out with Miss Snowdie's cross!" Later on, when Miss Snowdie finally had to sell the house and move away, her mother said, "Well, I see Snowdie gave up." When she told bad news, she wore a perfectly blank face and her voice was helpless and automatic, as if she repeated a lesson.

Virgie told on Mr. Voight too, but she had nobody to believe her, and so Miss Eckhart did not lose any pupils by that. Virgie did not know how to tell anything.

And for what Mr. Voight did there were no ready words—what would you call it? "Call it spontaneous combustion," Cassie's mother said. Some performances of people stayed partly untold for lack of a name, Cassie believed, as well as for lack of believers. Mr. Voight before so very long—it happened during a sojourn home of Mr. MacLain, she remembered—was transferred to travel another seven states, ending the problem; and yet Mr. Voight had done something that amounted to more than going naked under his robe and calling alarm like a turkey gobbler, it was more belligerent; and the least describable thing of all had been a look on his face; that was strange. Thinking of it now, and here in her room, Cassie found she had bared her teeth and set them, trying out the frantic look. She could not now, any more than then, really describe Mr. Voight, but without thinking she could *be* Mr. Voight, which was more frightening still.

Like a dreamer dreaming with reservations, Cassie moved over and changed the color for her scarf and moved back to the window. She reached behind her for a square of heavenly-hash in its platter and bit down on the marshmallow.

There was another man Miss Eckhart had been scared of, up until the last. (Not Mr. King MacLain. They always passed without touching, like two stars, perhaps they had some kind of eclipse-effect on each other.) She had been sweet on Mr. Hal Sissum, who clerked in the shoe department of Spights' store.

Cassie remembered him—who didn't know Mr. Sissum and all the Sissums? His sandy hair, parted on the side, shook over his ear like a toboggan cap when he ambled forward, in his long lazy step, to wait on people. He teased people that came to buy shoes, as though that took the prize for the vainest, most outlandish idea that could ever come over human beings.

Miss Eckhart had pretty ankles for a heavy lady like herself. Mrs. Stark said what a surprise it was for Miss Eckhart, of all people, to turn up with such pretty ankles, which made it the same as if she didn't have them. When she came in she took her seat and put her foot earnestly up on Mr. Sissum's stool like any other lady in Morgana and he spoke to her very nicely. He generally invited the bigger ladies, like Miss Nell Loomis or Miss Gert Bowles, to sit in the children's chair, but he held back, with Miss Eckhart, and spoke very nicely to her about her feet and treated them as a real concern; he even brought out a choice of shoes. To most ladies he brought out one box and said, "There's your shoe," as though shoes were something predestined. He knew them all so well.

Miss Eckhart might have come over to his aisle more often, but she had an incomprehensible habit of buying shoes two or even four pairs at a time, to save going back, or to take precaution against never finding them again. She didn't know how to do about Mr. Sissum at all.

But what could they either one have done? They couldn't go to church together; the Sissums were Presbyterians from the beginning of time and Miss Eckhart belonged to some distant church with a previously unheard-of name, the Lutheran. She could not go to the picture show with Mr. Sissum because he was already at the picture show. He played the music there every evening after the store closed—he had to; this was before the Bijou afforded a piano, and he could play the cello. He could not have refused Mr. Syd Sissum, who bought the stable and built the Bijou.

Virgie ran under the swingers.

Miss Eckhart used to come to the political speakings in the Starks' yard when Mr. Sissum played with the visiting band. Anybody could see him all evening then, high on the fresh plank platform behind his cello. Miss Eckhart, the true musician, sat on the damp night grass and listened. Nobody ever saw them really together any more than that. How did they know she was sweet on Mr. Sissum? But they did.

Mr. Sissum was drowned in the Big Black River one summer—fell out of his boat, all alone.

Cassie would rather remember the sweet soft speaking-nights in the Starks' yard. Before the speakings began, while the music was playing, Virgie and her older brother Victor ran wild all over everywhere, assaulting the crowd, where couples and threes and fives of people joined hands like paperdoll strings and wandered laughing and turning under the blossoming China trees and the heavy crape myrtles that were wound up in honeysuckle. How delicious it all smelled! Virgie let herself go completely, as anyone would like to do. Jinny Love Stark's swing was free to anybody and Virgie ran under the swingers, or jumped on behind, booting and pumping. She ran under sweethearts' twining arms, and nobody, even her brother, could catch her. She rolled the country people's watermelons away. She caught lightning bugs and tore out their lights for jewelry. She never rested as long as the music played except at last to throw herself hard and panting on the ground, her open mouth smiling against the trampled clover. Sometimes she made Victor climb up on the Starks' statue. Cassie remembered him, white face against dark leaves, a baseball cap turned backwards with the bill behind, and long black-stockinged legs wound over the snowy limbs of the goddess, and slowly, proudly sliding down.

But Virgie would not even watch him. She whirled in one direction till she fell down drunk, or turned about more slowly when they played *Vienna Woods*. She pushed Jinny Love Stark into her own lily bed. And all the time, she was eating. She ate all the ice cream she wanted. Now and then, in the soft parts of *Carmen* or before the storm in *William Tell*—even during dramatic pauses in the speaking—Mrs. Ice Cream Rainey's voice could be heard quickly calling, "Ice cream?" She had brought a freezer or two on Mr. Rainey's wagon to the foot of the yard. This time of year it might be fig. Sometimes Virgie whirled around with a fig ice cream cone in each hand, held poised like daggers.

Virgie would run closer and closer circles around Miss Eckhart, who sat alone (her mother never came out that far) on a *Bugle*, all four pages unfolded on the grass, listening. Up above, Mr. Sissum—who bent over his cello in the Bijou every night like an old sewing woman over the machine, like a shoe clerk over another foot to fit—shone in a Palm Beach coat and played straight-backed in the visiting band, and as fast as they did. The lock of hair was no longer hiding his eyes and nose; like the candidate for supervisor, he looked out.

Virgie put a loop of clover chain down over Miss Eckhart's head, her hat—her one hat—and all. She hung Miss Eckhart with flowers, while Mr. Sissum plucked the strings up above her. Miss Eckhart sat on, perfectly still and submissive. She gave no sign. She let the clover chain come down and lie on her breast.

Virgie laughed delightedly and with her long chain in her hand ran around and around her, binding her up with clovers. Miss Eckhart let her head roll back, and then Cassie felt that the teacher was filled with terror, perhaps with pain. She found it so easy—ever since Virgie showed her—to feel terror and pain in an outsider; in someone you did not know at all well, pain made you wonderfully sorry. It was not so easy to be sorry about it in the people close to you—it came unwillingly; and how strange—in yourself, on nights like this, pain—even a moment's pain—seemed inconceivable.

Cassie's whole family would be at the speakings, of course, her father moving at large through the crowd or sometimes sitting on the platform with Mr. Carmichael and Mr. Comus Stark with the rolling head and Mr. Spights. Cassie would try to stay in sight of her mother, but no matter how slightly she strayed, only to follow Virgie around the back-yard and find croquet balls in the grass, or down the hill to get a free cone, when she got back to their place her mother would be gone. She always lost her mother. She would find Loch there, rolled in a ball asleep in his sailor suit, his cheek holding down the ribbon of her softly removed hat. When she was back again, "I've just been through yonder to speak to my candidate," she said. "It's you that vanishes, Lady Bug, you that gets away."

It appeared to Cassie that only the figure of Miss Eckhart, off there like a vast receptacle in its island of space, did not move or sway when the band played *Tales of Hoffmann.*

One time Mr. Sissum gave Miss Eckhart something, a Billikin. The Billikin was a funny, ugly doll that Spights' store gave free to children with every pair of Billikin shoes. Never had Miss Eckhart laughed so hard, and with such an unfamiliar sound, as she laughed to see Mr. Sissum's favor. Tears ran down her bright, distorted cheeks every time one of the children coming into the studio picked the Billikin up. When her laughter was exhausted she would sigh faintly and ask for the doll, and then soberly set it down on a little minaret table, as if it were a vase of fresh red roses. Her old mother took it one day and cracked it across her knee.

When Mr. Sissum was drowned, Miss Eckhart came to his funeral like everybody else. The Loomises invited her to ride with them. She looked exactly the same as ever, round and solid, her back a ramrod in her dress that was the wrong season's length and her same hat, the home-made one with cambric flowers sticking up on it. But when the coffin was lowered into Mr. Sissum's place in the Sissum lot under a giant magnolia tree, and Mr. Sissum's preacher, Dr. Carlyle, said burial service, Miss Eckhart broke out of the circle.

42

She pressed to the front, through Sissums from everywhere and all the Presbyterians, and went close to get a look; and if Dr. Loomis had not caught her she would have gone headlong into the red clay hole. People said she might have thrown herself upon the coffin if they'd let her; just as, later, Miss Katie Rainey did on Victor's when he was brought back from France. But Cassie had the impression that Miss Eckhart simply wanted to see—to see what was being done with Mr. Sissum.

As she struggled, her round face seemed stretched wider than it was long by a feeling that failed to match the feelings of everybody else. It was not the same as sorrow. Miss Eckhart, a stranger to their cemetery, where none of her people lay, pushed forward with her unstylish, winter purse swinging on her arm, and began to nod her head—sharply, to one side and then the other. She appeared almost little under the tree, but Mr. Comus Stark and Dr. Loomis looked more shrunken still by the side of her as they—sent by ladies—reached for her elbows. Her vigorous nods included them too, increasing in urgency. It was the way she nodded at pupils to bring up their rhythm, helping out the metronome.

Cassie remembered how Miss Snowdie MacLain's grip tightened on her hand and stayed tightened until Miss Eckhart got over it. But Cassie remembered her manners better than to seem to watch Miss Eckhart after one look; she stared down at her Billikin shoes. And her mother had slipped away.

It was strange that in Mr. Sissum's life Miss Eckhart, as everybody said, had never known what to do; and now she did this. Her sharp nodding was like something to encourage them all—to say that she knew now, to do this, and that nobody need speak to her or touch her unless, if they thought best, they could give her this little touch at the elbows, the steer of politeness.

"*Pizzicato.*"

Once, Miss Eckhart gave out the word to define in the catechism lesson.

"*Pizzicato* is when Mr. Sissum played the cello before he got drowned."

That was herself: Cassie heard her own words. She had tried—she was as determined as if she'd been dared—to see how that sounded, spoken out like that to Miss Eckhart's face. She remembered how Miss Eckhart listened to her and did nothing but sit still as a statue, as she sat when the flowers came down over her head.

After the way she cried in the cemetery—for they decided it must have been crying she did—some ladies stopped their little girls from learning any more music; Miss Jefferson Moody stopped Parnell.

Cassie heard noises—a thump next door, the antiquated sound of thunder. There was nothing she could see—only Old Man Holifield's hat that idly made a half-turn on the bedpost, as if something, by a long grapevine, had jolted it.

One summer morning, a sudden storm had rolled up and three children were caught at the studio—Virgie Rainey, little Jinny Love Stark, and Cassie—though the two bigger girls might have run their short way home with newspapers over their hair.

Miss Eckhart, without saying what she was going to do, poked her finger solidly along the pile of music on top of the piano, pulled out a piece, and sat down on her own stool. It was the only time she ever performed in Cassie's presence except when she took the other half in duets.

Miss Eckhart played as if it were Beethoven; she struck the music open midway and it was in soft yellow tatters like old satin. The thunder rolled and Miss Eckhart frowned and bent forward or she leaned back to play; at moments her solid body swayed from side to side like a tree trunk.

44

The piece was so hard that she made mistakes and repeated to correct them, so long and stirring that it soon seemed longer than the day itself had been, and in playing it Miss Eckhart assumed an entirely different face. Her skin flattened and drew across her cheeks, her lips changed. The face could have belonged to someone else—not even to a woman, necessarily. It was the face a mountain could have, or what might be seen behind the veil of a waterfall. There in the rainy light it was a sightless face, one for music only—though the fingers kept slipping and making mistakes they had to correct. And if the sonata had an origin in a place on earth, it was the place where Virgie, even, had never been and was not likely ever to go.

The music came with greater volume—with fewer halts—and Jinny Love tiptoed forward and began turning the music. Miss Eckhart did not even see her—her arm struck the child, making a run. Coming from Miss Eckhart, the music made all the pupils uneasy, almost alarmed; something had burst out, unwanted, exciting, from the wrong person's life. This was some brilliant thing too splendid for Miss Eckhart, piercing and striking the air around her the way a Christmas firework might almost jump out of the hand that was, each year, inexperienced anew.

It was when Miss Eckhart was young that she had learned this piece, Cassie divined. Then she had almost forgotten it. But it took only a summer rain to start it again; she had been pricked and the music came like the red blood under the scab of a forgotten fall. The little girls, all stationed about the studio with the rushing rain outside, looked at one another, the three quite suddenly on some equal footing. They were all wondering—thinking—perhaps about escape. A mosquito circled Cassie's head, singing, and fastened on her arm, but she dared not move.

What Miss Eckhart might have told them a long time ago was that there was more than the ear could bear to hear or the eye to see, even in her. The music was too much for Cassie Morrison. It lay in the very

There in the rainy light it was a sightless face, one for music only.

heart of the stormy morning—there was something almost too violent about a storm in the morning. She stood back in the room with her whole body averted as if to ward off blows from Miss Eckhart's strong left hand, her eyes on the faintly winking circle of the safe in the wall. She began to think of an incident that had happened to Miss Eckhart instead of about the music she was playing; that was one way.

One time, at nine o'clock at night, a crazy Negro had jumped out of the school hedge and got Miss Eckhart, had pulled her down and threatened to kill her. That was long ago. She had been walking by herself after dark; nobody had told her any better. When Dr. Loomis made her well, people were surprised that she and her mother did not move away. They wished she had moved away, everybody but poor Miss Snowdie; then they wouldn't always have to remember that a terrible thing once happened to her. But Miss Eckhart stayed, as though she considered one thing not so much more terrifying than another. (After all, nobody knew why she came!) It was because she was from so far away, at any rate, people said to excuse her, that she couldn't comprehend; Miss Perdita Mayo, who took in sewing and made everybody's trousseaux, said Miss Eckhart's *differences* were why shame alone had not killed her and killed her mother too; that differences were reasons.

Cassie thought as she listened, had to listen, to the music that perhaps more than anything it was the terrible fate that came on her that people could not forgive Miss Eckhart for. Yet things divined and endured, spectacular moments, hideous things like the black stranger jumping out of the hedge at nine o'clock, all seemed to Cassie to be by their own nature rising—and so alike—and crossing the sky and setting, the way the planets did. Or they were more like whole constellations, turning at their very centers maybe, like Perseus and Orion and Cassiopeia in her Chair and the Big Bear and Little Bear, maybe often upside down, but terribly recognizable. It was not just the sun and moon that traveled. In the deepening of the night, the rising sky lifted like a cover when Louella let it soar as she made the bed.

All kinds of things would rise and set in your own life, you could begin now to watch for them, roll back your head and feel their rays come down and reach your open eyes.

Performing, Miss Eckhart was unrelenting. Even when the worst of the piece was over, her fingers like foam on rocks pulled at the spent-out part with unstilled persistence, insolence, violence.

Then she dropped her hands.

"Play it again, Miss Eckhart!" they all cried in startled recoil, begging for the last thing they wanted, looking at her great lump of body.

"No."

Jinny Love Stark gave them a grown-up look and closed the music. When she did, the other two saw it wasn't the right music at all, for it was some bound-together songs of Hugo Wolf.

"What were you playing, though?"

That was Miss Snowdie MacLain, standing in the door, holding streams of bead curtains in both hands.

"I couldn't say," Miss Eckhart said, rising. "I have forgotten."

The pupils all ran out in the slackening rain without another word, scattering in three directions by the mimosa tree, its flowers like wet fur, which once grew in the yard of the now-vacant house.

Für Elise. It came again, but in a labored, foolish way. Was it a man, using one finger?

Virgie Rainey had gone straight from taking music to playing the piano in the picture show. With her customary swiftness and lightness she had managed to skip an interval, some world-in-between where Cassie and Missie and Parnell were, all dyeing scarves. Virgie had gone direct into the world of power and emotion, which was beginning to seem even bigger than they had all thought. She belonged now with the Gish and the Talmadge sisters. With her yellow pencil she hit the tin plate when the tent opened where Valentino lived.

Virgie sat nightly at the foot of the screen ready for all that happened at the Bijou, and keeping pace with it. Nothing proved too much for her or ever got too far ahead, as it certainly got ahead of Mr. Sissum. When the dam broke everywhere at once, or when Nazimova cut off both feet with a saber rather than face life with Sinji, Virgie was instantly playing *Kamennoi-Ostrow.* Missie Spights said only one thing was wrong with having Virgie to play at the Bijou. She didn't work hard enough. Some evenings, she would lean back in her chair and let a whole forest fire burn in dead silence on the screen, and then when the sweethearts had found each other, she would switch on her light with a loud click and start up with creeping, minor runs—perhaps *Anitra's Dance.* But that had nothing to do with working hard.

The only times she played *Für Elise* now were for the advertisements; she played it moodily while the slide of the big white chicken on the watermelon-pink sky came on for Bowles' Gro., or the yellow horn on the streaky blue sky flashed on for the *Bugle,* with Cassie's father's picture as a young man inserted in the wavy beam of noise. *Für Elise* never got finished any more; it began, went a little way, and was interrupted by Virgie's own clamorous hand. She could do things with "You've Got to See Mama Every Night," and "Avalon."

By now, it was not likely she could play the opening movement of her Liszt concerto. That was the piece none of the rest of them could ever hope to play. Virgie would be heard from in the world, playing that, Miss Eckhart said, revealing to children with one ardent cry her lack of knowledge of the world. How could Virgie be heard from, in the world? And "the world"! Where did Miss Eckhart think she was now? Virgie Rainey, she repeated over and over, had a gift, and she must go away from Morgana. From them all. From her studio. In the world, she must study and practice her music for the rest of her life. In repeating all this, Miss Eckhart suffered.

And all the time, it was on Miss Eckhart's piano that Virgie had to

do her practicing. The Raineys' old borrowed piano was butted and
half-eaten by the goats one summer day; something that could only
happen at the Raineys'. But they had all known Virgie would never go,
or study, or practice anywhere, never would even have her own piano,
because it wouldn't be like her. They felt no less sure of that when they
heard, every recital, every June, Virgie Rainey playing better and
better something that was harder and harder, or watched this fill Miss
Eckhart with stiff delight, curious anguish. The very place to prove Miss
Eckhart crazy was on her own subject, piano playing: she didn't know
what she was talking about.

When the Raineys, after their barn got blown away in a big wind,
had no more money to throw away on piano lessons, Miss Eckhart said
she would teach Virgie free, because she must not stop learning. But
later she made her pick the figs off the trees in the backyard in summer
and the pecans off the ground in the front yard in winter, for her lessons. Virgie said Miss Eckhart never gave her a one. Yet she always
had nuts in her pocket.

Cassie heard a banging and a running next door, the obvious sound
of falling. She shut her eyes.

"Virgie Rainey, *danke schoen*." Once that was said in a dreadful
voice, condemning. There were times in the studio when Miss Eckhart's mother would roll in; she had a wheelchair. The first years, she
had kept to herself, rolling around no closer than the dining room,
round and round with a whining wheel. She was old, and fair as a doll.
Up close, her yellowish hair was powdery like goldenrod that had gone
forgotten in a vase, turned white in its curls like Miss Snowdie's. She
had wasting legs that showed knifelike down her long skirt, and
clumsy-shaped, suffering feet that she placed just so out in front of her
on the step of her chair, as if she wanted you to think they were pretty.

The mother rolled into the studio whenever she liked, as time went on; with her shepherdess curls she bobbed herself through the beads that opened to her easier than a door. She would roll a certain distance into the room, then stop the wheels and wait there. She was not so much listening to the lesson as watching it, and though she was not keeping time, it was all the more noticeable the way her hands would tip, tap against her chair; she had a brass thimble on one finger.

Ordinarily, Miss Eckhart never seemed disturbed by her mother's abrupt visits. She appeared gentler, more bemused than before, when old Mrs. Eckhart made Parnell Moody cry, just by looking at Parnell too hard. Should daughters *forgive* mothers (with mothers under their heel)? Cassie would rather look at the two of them at night, separated by the dark and the distance between. For when from your own table you saw the Eckharts through their window in the light of a lamp, and Miss Eckhart with a soundless ebullience bouncing up to wait on her mother, sometimes you could imagine them back far away from Morgana, before they had troubles and before they had come to you— plump, bright, and sweet somewhere.

Once when Virgie was practicing on Miss Eckhart's piano, and before she was through, the old mother screamed, "*Danke schoen, danke schoen, danke schoen!*" Cassie heard and saw her.

She screamed with a shy look still on her face, as though through Virgie Rainey she would scream at the whole world, at least at all the music in the world and wasn't that all right? Then she sat there looking out the front window, half smiling, having mocked her daughter. Virgie, of course, kept on practicing—it was a Schumann "forest piece." She had a pomegranate flower (the marbleized kind, from the Moodys') stuck in her breast-pin, and it did not even move.

But when the song was smoothly finished, Miss Eckhart made her way among the little tables and chairs across the studio. Cassie thought she was going for a drink of water, or something for herself. When she reached her mother, Miss Eckhart slapped the side of her mouth. She stood there a moment more, leaning over the chair—while it seemed to Cassie that it must, after all, have been the mother that slapped the daughter—with the key from her bosom, slipped out, beginning to swing on its chain, back and forth, catching the light.

Then Miss Eckhart, with her back turned, asked Cassie and Virgie to stay for dinner.

Enveloping all that the pupils did—entering the house, parting the curtains, turning the music page, throwing up the wrist for a "rest"—was the smell of cooking. But the smell was wrong, as the pitch of a note could be wrong. It was the smell of food nobody else had ever tasted.

Cabbage was cooked there by no Negro and by no way it was ever cooked in Morgana. With wine. The wine was brought on foot by Dago Joe, and to the front door. Some nice mornings the studio smelled like a spiced apple. But it was known from Mr. Wiley Bowles, the grocer, that Miss Eckhart and her mother (whose mouth was still held crooked after the slap) ate pigs' brains. Poor Miss Snowdie!

Cassie yearned—she did want to taste the cabbage—that was really the insurmountable thing, and even the brains of a pig she would have put in her mouth that day. With that, Missie Spights might be flouted. But when Miss Eckhart said, "Please—please, will you stay to dinner?" Virgie and Cassie twined arms and said "No" together.

The war came and all through it and even after 1918 people said Miss Eckhart was a German and still wanted the Kaiser to win, and that Miss Snowdie could get along without her. But the old mother died, and Miss Snowdie said Miss Eckhart needed a friendly roof more than she did herself. Miss Eckhart raised the price of her lessons to six dollars a month. Miss Mamie Carmichael stopped her girls from taking, for this or for one thing or another, and then Miss Billy Texas Spights stopped Missie to be like her. Virgie stopped taking her free lessons when her brother Victor was killed in France, but that might have been coincidence, for Virgie had a birthday: she was fourteen. It might have been Virgie's stopping that took away Miss Eckhart's luck for good.

And when she stopped, Virgie's hand lost its touch—that was what they said. Perhaps nobody wanted Virgie Rainey to be anything in Morgana any more than they had wanted Miss Eckhart to be, and they were the two of them still linked together by people's saying that. How much might depend on people's being linked together? Even Miss Snowdie had a little harder time than she had had already with Ran and Scooter, her bad boys, by being linked with roomers and music lessons and Germans.

The time came when Miss Eckhart had almost no pupils at all. Then she had only Cassie.

Her mother, Cassie had long known in her heart, could not help but despise Miss Eckhart. It was just for living so close to her, or maybe just for living, a poor unwanted teacher and unmarried. And Cassie's instinct told her her mother despised herself for despising. That was why she kept Cassie taking just a little longer after Miss Eckhart had been deserted by all the other mothers. It was more that than the money, which would go to Miss Snowdie on the rent bill. The child had to make up for her mother's abhorrence, to keep her mother as kind as she really was. While Miss Snowdie could stay kind through always being far away in her heart.

Cassie herself was well applauded when she played a piece. The recital audience always clapped more loudly for her than they did for Virgie; but then they clapped more loudly still for little Jinny Love Stark. It was Cassie who was awarded the Presbyterian Church's music scholarship that year to go to college—not Virgie. It made Cassie feel "natural"; winning the scholarship over Virgie did not surprise her too much. The only reason for that which she put into words, to be self-effacing, was that the Raineys were Methodists; and yet she did not, basically, understand a slight. And now stretching ahead of her, as far as she could see, were those yellow Schirmer books: all the rest of her life.

But Miss Eckhart sent for Virgie and gave her a present that Cassie for many days could close her eyes and see. It was a little butterfly pin made of cut-out silver, like silver lace, to wear on her shoulder; the safety-catch wasn't any good.

But that didn't make Virgie say she loved Miss Eckhart or go on practicing as she told her. Miss Eckhart gave Virgie an armful of books that were written in German about the lives of the masters, and Virgie couldn't read a word; and Mr. Fate Rainey tore out the Venusberg pictures and fed them to the pigs. Miss Eckhart tried all those things and was strict to the last in the way she gave all her love to Virgie Rainey and none to anybody else, the way she was strict in music; and for Miss Eckhart love was just as arbitrary and one-sided as music teaching.

Her love never did anybody any good.

Then one day, Miss Eckhart had to move out.

The trouble was that Miss Snowdie had had to sell the house. She moved with her two boys back to MacLain where she came from, seven miles away, and where her husband's people came from too. She sold the house to Mrs. Vince Murphy. And soon Miss Eckhart was put out, with Mrs. Vince Murphy retaining the piano and anything Miss Eckhart had or that Miss Snowdie had left for Miss Eckhart.

It was not long before Mrs. Vince Murphy was struck by lightning and left the house to Miss Francine, who always kept meaning to fix up the house and take boarders, but had a beau then. She temporized by putting Mr. Holifield in to see that nobody ran off with the bathtubs and what furniture there was. And the house "ran down"—as they said alike of houses and clocks, thought Cassie, to put the seal on inferiority and carelessness and fainting hopes alike, and for ever.

Then stories began to be told of what Miss Eckhart had really done to her old mother. People said the old mother had been in pain for years, and nobody was told. What kind of pain they did not say. But they said that during the war, when Miss Eckhart lost pupils and they did not have very much to eat, she would give her mother paregoric to make sure she slept all night and not wake the street with noise or complaint, for fear still more pupils would be taken away. Some people said Miss Eckhart killed her mother with opium.

Miss Eckhart, in a room out at the old Holifields' on Morgan's Wood Road, got older and weaker, though not noticeably thinner, and would be seen from time to time walking into Morgana, up one side of the street and down the other and home. People said you could look at her and see she had broken. Yet she still had authority. She could still stop young, unknowing children like Loch on the street and ask them imperative questions, "Where were you throwing that ball?" "Are you trying to break that tree?". . . Of course her only associates from first to last were children; not counting Miss Snowdie.

Where did Miss Eckhart come from, and where in the end did she go? In Morgana most destinies were known to everybody and seemed to go without saying. It was unlikely that anybody except Miss Perdita Mayo had asked Miss Eckhart where the Eckharts came from, where exactly in the world, and so received the answer. And Miss Perdita was so undependable: she couldn't tell you now, to save her life. And Miss Eckhart had gone down out of sight.

Once on a Sunday ride, Cassie's father said he bet a nickel that was old lady Eckhart hoeing peas out there on the County Farm, and he bet another nickel she could still do the work of ten nigger men.

Wherever she was, she had no people. Surely, by this time, she had nobody at all. The only one she had ever wanted to have for "people" was Virgie Rainey *Danke schoen*.

Missie Spights said that if Miss Eckhart had allowed herself to be called by her first name, then she would have been like other ladies. Or if Miss Eckhart had belonged to a church that had ever been heard of, and the ladies would have had something to invite her to belong to . . . Or if she had been married to anybody at all, just the awfullest man—like Miss Snowdie MacLain, that everybody could feel sorry for.

Cassie knelt, and with hurrying hands untied all the knots in her scarf. She held it out in a square. Though she was not thinking of her scarf, it did surprise her; she didn't see indeed how she had ever made it. They had told her so. She hung it over the two posts of a chair to dry and as it fell softly over the ladder of the back she thought that somewhere, even up to the last, there could have been for Miss Eckhart a little opening wedge—a crack in the door. . . .

But if I had been the one to see it open, she thought slowly, I might have slammed it tight for ever. I might.

Her eyes lifted to the window where she saw a thin gray streak go down, like the trail of a match. The humming-bird! She knew him, one that came back every year. She stood and looked down at him. He was a little emerald bobbin, suspended as always before the opening four-o'clocks. Metallic and misty together, tangible and intangible, splendid and fairy-like, the haze of his invisible wings mysterious, like the ring around the moon—had anyone ever tried to catch him? Not she. Let him be suspended there for a moment each year for a hundred years—incredibly thirsty, greedy for every drop in every four-o'clock trumpet in the yard, as though he had them numbered—then dart.

"Like a military operation."

Cassie's father always said the recital was planned that way, in all its tactics and dress. The preparations went on for many hot, secret weeks—all of May. "You're not to tell anyone what the program is to be," Miss Eckhart warned at every lesson and rehearsal, as if there were other music teachers, other classes, rivaling, and as if every year the program didn't begin with "The Stubborn Rocking Horse" by the one boy and end with *Marche Militaire* for eight hands. What Virgie played in the recital one year, Cassie (gradually improving) would come to the next, and Missie Spights had it one more step in the future.

Miss Eckhart decided early in the spring what color each child should wear, with what color sash and hair ribbon, and sent written word to the mother. She explained to the children that it was important which color followed which. "Think of God's rainbow and its order," and she would shake her pencil in abrupt little beats in an arch overhead; but they had to think of Spights' store. The quartet, with four dresses in view at one time and in close conjunction, pushing one another, made Miss Eckhart especially apprehensive.

Account was kept in a composition book of each child's assigned color; Miss Eckhart made a little "v" beside the name in token of the mother's agreement and regarded it as a promise. When the dress was reported finished, starched, and ironed, a line was drawn through that name.

In general, mothers were scared of Miss Eckhart then. Miss Lizzie Stark laughed about it, but she was as scared as anybody else. Miss Eckhart assumed that there would be a new dress for every pupil for the recital night, that Miss Perdita Mayo would make it, or if not Miss Perdita, who even with her sister could not make them all, then the pupil's own mother. The dress must be made with the fingers and the edges of bertha and flounce picoted, the sash as well; and—whatever happened—the costume must be saved for recital night. And this was the kind of thing that both Miss Perdita and most mothers understood immediately.

And it could seldom be worn again; certainly not to another recital—by then an "old" dress. A recital dress was fuller and had more trimming than a Sunday dress. It was like a flower girl's dress in a wedding; once little Nina Carmichael's *was* a flower girl's dress, after Etta's wedding, but this was special dispensation. The dress should be organdie, with ruffles on skirt, bertha, and sleeves; it called for a satin or taffeta sash tied in a back bow with long tails, pointed like the tails of arrows, to hang over the stool and, if it could be afforded, to reach the floor.

All through May, Miss Eckhart would ask how far along the dresses had come. Cassie was uneasy, for her mother's way was to speak too late for Miss Perdita's list and plan to run the dress up herself at the last minute; but Cassie had to encourage Miss Eckhart. "She's just evening my hem," she would report, when the material would still be lying folded up with the newspaper-pattern borrowed from Miss Jefferson Moody, in the *armoire*.

As for the program, that was no problem; it existed readymade without discussion. Far back in the winter, Virgie Rainey would have been allotted a piece that was the most difficult Miss Eckhart could find in the music cabinet. Sometimes it was not as showy a thing as Teensie Loomis always had to have (before she got old and stopped taking), but always it was the hardest piece of all. It would be the test of what Virgie could do, to learn it; an ordeal was set for her each year and each year it was accomplished, with no yielding sign from Virgie that she had struggled. The rest of the program would lead up to this, and did not matter enough to be altered seriously from one year to the next. Just so everybody had a piece to play, and a new dress finished in time, and kept the secrets, there was nothing to do but endure May.

A week ahead of the night, the gold chairs were set in a solid row across the room, to look as if all were gold, and the extra chairs would appear one by one behind them until the room was filled. Miss Eckhart must have carried them in from the dining room first, and then, as she could get hold of them, from elsewhere. She carried them downstairs from Miss Snowdie's freely, of course, and then even from Mr. Voight's, for no matter what Miss Eckhart thought of Mr. Voight, she wouldn't hesitate to go in and take his chairs for the recital.

A second piano had to be rented from the Presbyterian Sunday

School (through the Starks), hauled over in time for rehearsing the quartet all together, and of course tuned. There were programs to be printed (through the Morrisons), elaborate enough to include the opus numbers, the first, middle, and last name of each pupil, and flowing across the top in a script which resembled, as if for a purpose, Miss Eckhart's writing in the monthly bills, the full name of Miss Lotte Elisabeth Eckhart. Some little untalented Maloney would give the programs out at the door from a pink fruit plate.

On the day, gladiolas or carnations in princess-baskets were expected to arrive for each child, duly ordered from some Loomis florist-connections in Vicksburg and kept in buckets of water on the MacLains' shady back porch. They would be presented at the proper time—immediately after the bow—by Miss Eckhart. The pupil could hold the basket for the count of three—this had been rehearsed, using a black umbrella—then present it back to Miss Eckhart, who had in mind a crescent moon design on the floor which she would fill in basket by basket on the night. Jinny Love Stark always received a bouquet of Parma violets in a heart of leaves, and had to be allowed to keep it. She said, "Ta-ta." She never did give it up a single year, which hurt the effect.

For the recital was, after all, a ceremony. Better than school's being let out—for that presupposed examinations—or the opening political fireworks—the recital celebrated June. Both dread and delight were to come down on little girls that special night, when only certain sashes and certain flowers could possibly belong, and with only smart, pretty little girls to carry things out.

And Miss Eckhart pushed herself to quite another level of life for it. A blushing sensitivity sprang up in her every year at the proper time like a flower of the season, like the Surprise Lilies that came up with no leaves and overnight in Miss Nell's yard. Miss Eckhart stirred here and there, utterly carried away by matters that at other times interested her least—dresses and sashes, prominence and precedence, smiles and bows. It was strange, exciting. She called up the pictures on those little square party invitations, the brown bear in a frill and the black poodle standing on a chair to shave at a mirror. . . .

With recital night over, the sensitivity and the drive too would be over and gone. But then all trials would be ended. The limitless part of vacation would have come. Girls and boys could go barefooted alike in the mornings.

The night of the recital was always clear and hot; everyone came. The prospective audience turned out in full oppression.

Miss Eckhart and her pupils were not yet to be visible. It was up to Miss Snowdie MacLain to be at the door, and she was at the door, staunchly, as if she'd been in on things the whole time. She welcomed all female Morgana there in perfect innocence. By eight o'clock the studio was packed.

Miss Katie Rainey would always come early. She trembled with delight, like a performer herself, and she had milked with that hat on. She laughed with pleasure as she grew accustomed to it all, and through the recital she would stay much in evidence, the first to clap when a piece was over, and pleased equally with the music she listened to and the gold chair she sat on. And Old Man Fate Rainey, the butter-milk man, was the only father who came. He remained standing. Miss Perdita Mayo, who had made most of the recital dresses, was always on the front row to see that the bastings had all been pulled out after the dresses got home, and beside her was Miss Hattie Mayo, her quiet sister who helped her.

As the studio filled, Cassie, peeping around the sheet curtain (*they* were all herded in the dining room), bore the dread that her mother might not come at all. She was always late, perhaps because she lived so near. Miss Lizzie Stark, the most important mother there, who was just waiting for Jinny Love to get a little older to play better, would turn around in her chair down front to spot each of the other mothers. Knowing that too, and dressed beautifully in a becoming flowery dress just right for a mother on recital night, Cassie's mother could not walk across the two yards on time to save her life. And Cassie's *Rustle of Spring*, for instance, was very hard, harder than Missie Spights' piece; but it appeared that everything Miss Eckhart planned for, Cassie's mother could let go for nothing.

In the studio decorated like the inside of a candy box, with "material" scalloping the mantel shelf and doilies placed under every movable object, now thus made immovable, with streamers of white ribbons and nosegays of pink and white Maman Cochet roses and the last MacLain sweetpeas dividing and re-dividing the room, it was as hot as fire. No matter that this was the first night of June; no electric fans were to whir around while music played. The metronome, ceremoniously closed, stood on the piano like a vase. There was no piece of music anywhere in sight.

When the first unreasoning hush—there was the usual series—fell over the audience, the room seemed to shake with the agitation of palmetto and feather fans alone, plus the occasional involuntary tick of the metronome within its doors. There was the mixture together of agitation and decoration which could make every little forthcoming child turn pale with a kind of ultimate dizziness. Whoever might look up at the ceiling for surcease would be floundered within a paper design stemming out of the chandelier, as complicated and as unavailing as a cut-out paper snowflake.

Now Miss Eckhart came into the room all changed, with her dark hair pulled low on her brow, and gestured for silence. She was wearing her recital dress, which made her look larger and closer-to than she looked at any other times. It was an old dress: Miss Eckhart disregarded her own rules. People would forget that dress between times

61

and then she would come out in it again, the untidy folds not quite spotlessly clean, gathered about her bosom and falling heavy as a coat to the sides; it was a tawny crepe-back satin. There was a bodice of browning lace. It was as rich and hot and deep-looking as a furskin. The unexpected creamy flesh on her upper arms gave her a look of emerging from it.

Miss Eckhart, achieving silence, stood in the shadowy spot directly under the chandelier. Her feet, white-shod, shod by Mr. Sissum for good, rested in the chalk circle previously marked on the floor and now, she believed, perfectly erased. One hand, with its countable little muscles so hard and ready, its stained, blue nails, went to the other hand and they folded quite still, holding nothing, until they lost their force by lying on her breast and made a funny little house with peaks and gables. Standing near the piano but not near enough to help, she presided but not with her whole heart on guard against disaster; while disaster was what remained on the minds of the little girls. Starting with the youngest, she called them out.

So they played, and except Virgie, all played their worst. They shocked themselves. Parnell Moody burst into tears on schedule. But Miss Eckhart never seemed to notice or to care. How forgetful she seemed at exactly the moments she should have been agonized! You expected the whip, almost, for forgetting to repeat before the second ending, or for failing to count ten before you came around the curtain at all; and instead you received a strange smile. It was as though Miss Eckhart, at the last, were grateful to you for *anything*.

When Hilda Ray Bowles' turn came and Miss Eckhart herself was to bend down and move the stool out twelve inches, she did it in a spirit of gentle, uninterrupted abstraction. She might be not moving a stool out for an overgrown girl at all, but performing some gentle ministration to someone else, someone who was not there; perhaps it was Beethoven, who wrote Hilda Ray's piece, and perhaps not.

But recital night was Virgie's night, whatever else it was.

Cassie played, and her mother—not betraying her, after all—was seated among the rest. At the end, she had creased her program into a little hat, for which Cassie could have fallen at her feet.

But recital night was Virgie's night, whatever else it was. The time Virgie Rainey was most wonderful in her life, to Cassie, was when she came out—her turn was just before the quartet—wearing a Christmas-red satin band in her hair with rosettes over the ears, held on by a new elastic across the back; she had a red sash drawn around under the arms of a starched white swiss dress. She was thirteen. She played the *Fantasia on Beethoven's Ruins of Athens*, and when she finished and got up and made her bow, the red of the sash was all over the front of her waist, she was wet and stained as if she had been stabbed in the heart, and a delirious and enviable sweat ran down from her forehead and cheeks and she licked it in with her tongue.

Cassie, who had slipped around to the front, was spellbound still when Miss Katie Rainey put a hand on her sash and to her pure terror said, "Oh, but I wish Virgie had a sister!"

Then there was only the quartet, and with the last chord—sudden disintegration itself—laughter and teasing broke loose. All the children got a kiss or a token spank in congratulation and then ran free. Ladies waved and beckoned with their fans, conversation opened up. Flowers were lifted high, shown off, thrown, given, and pulled to giddy pieces by fingers freed for the summer. The MacLain twins, now crashing restraint, rushed downstairs in identical cowboy suits, pointing and even firing cap pistols. Two fans were set rumbling and walking on the floor, from which the dropped programs flew up like a flock of birds, while the decorations whipped and played all over. Neither piano was gone near except for punching out "Sally in Her Shimmie Tail." Little Jinny Stark, after all, fell, skinned her knee and bled profusely. It was like any other party.

"Punch and *Kuchen!*" Miss Eckhart came announcing.

The big MacLain dining room at the back, where Miss Snowdie only wintered her flowers for the most part, was thrown open tonight. Punch was being served from the MacLain punch bowl, one of Miss Snowdie's gifts from her husband—served impromptu by Miss Billy Texas Spights, who sprang for the ladle, and they drank it out of the twenty-four Mac-Lain cups and the twelve Loomis. The little cakes that Miss Eckhart tirelessly brought out were sweet, light, and warm, their tops sprinkled with colored "shot" that came (or so they'd thought) only out of glass pistols sold on trains. When the plate was empty you saw it was decorated with slipping flower garlands and rowdy babies, sprinkled with gold and now with golden crumbs.

Miss Eckhart's cheeks flooded with color as the guests accepted her sugar cookies and came back to lift their punch cups, with the drowned fruit in the bottom, again to her quick, brimming ladle. ("*I'll* give you more punch!" she cried, when Miss Billy Texas started counting.) Her hair was as low on her forehead as Circe's, on the fourth grade wall feeding her swine. She smiled, not on any particular one but on everyone, everywhere she looked and everywhere she went—for the party had spread out—from studio to dining room and back and out on the porch, where she called, "What is this out here? You little girls come back inside and stay till you eat my *Kuchen* all up! The last crumb!" It made them laugh to hear her, when strictness was only a pretense.

Miss Lizzie Stark, although she had occasionally referred to Miss Eckhart as "Miss Do-daddle," did not spare herself from wearing her most elaborate hat, one resembling a large wreath or a wedding cake, and it was constantly in the vision, turned this way and that like a floating balloon at a fair over the heads of the crowd. The canary sang; his cover was lifted off. Gradually the Maman Cochets bowed their little green stems over the vase's edge.

At the close of the evening, saying goodnight, people congratulated Miss Eckhart and her mother. Old Mrs. Eckhart had sat near the door during the whole evening—had sat by Miss Snowdie at the door, when she welcomed them in. She wore a dark dress too, but it was sprigged. In the path of the talking and laughing mothers and the now wild children she sat blinking her eyes, but amenable, like a baby when he is wheeled out into the sunlight. While Miss Snowdie watched her kindly, she would hold her mouth in one evening-long smile; she was letting herself be looked at and herself, at the end, be thanked.

Miss Eckhart, breasting the pushing, departing children, moving among the swinging princess-baskets and the dropped fans of the suddenly weakened mothers, would be heard calling, "Virgie Rainey? Virgie Rainey?" Then she would look down ceremoniously at the sleepiest and smallest child, who had only played "Playful Kittens" that night. All her pupils on that evening partook of the grace of Virgie Rainey. Miss Eckhart would catch them running out the door, speaking German to them and holding them to her. In the still night air her dress felt damp and spotted, as though she had run a long way.

Cassie listened, but *Für Elise* was not repeated. She took up her ukulele from the foot of the bed. She screwed it into tune and played it, slurring the chords expertly and fanning with her fingers. She strolled around her scarf hanging up to dry, playing a chorus or two, and then wandered back to the window.

There she saw Loch go hanging on all fours like a monkey down the hackberry limb. Far on the other side of the tree he hung by his hands, perfectly still, diver-like—not going into any of his tricks. That was the way he stayed in bed taking quinine.

He was concerned not with tricks but with watching something inside the vacant house. Loch could see in. Cassie opened her mouth to cry out, but the cry wouldn't come.

Except for once, she had not answered Loch all day when he called her, and now the sight of his spread-eagled back in the white night drawers seemed as far from her as the morning star. It was gone from her, any way to shield his innocence, when his innocence was out there shining at her, cavorting—for Loch calmly reversed himself and hung by his knees; plunged upside down, he looked in at the old studio window, with his pompadour cap falling to earth and his hair spiking out all over his young boy's head.

Once Loch wandered over their house in a skirt, beating on a christening cup with a pencil. "Mama, do you think I can ever play music too?" "Why, of course, dear heart. You're *my* child. Just you bide your time." (He was her favorite.) And he never could—bide or play. How Cassie had adored him! He didn't know one tune from another. "Is this *Jesus Loves Me?*" he'd ask, interrupting his own noise. She looked out at him now as stricken as if she saw him hurt, from long ago, and silently performing tricks to tell her. She stood there at her window. Softly she was playing and singing, "By the light, light, light, light, light of the silvery moon," her favorite song.

She could never go for herself, never creep out on the shimmering bridge of the tree, or reach the dark magnet there that drew you inside, kept drawing you in. She could not see herself do an unknown thing. She was not Loch, she was not Virgie Rainey; she was not her mother. She was Cassie in her room, seeing the knowledge and torment beyond her reach, standing at her window singing—in a voice soft, rather full today, and halfway thinking it was pretty.

III

After a moment of blackness, upside down, Loch opened his eyes. Nothing had happened. The house he watched was all silence but for the progressing tick-tock that was different from a clock's. There were outer sounds. His sister was practicing on her ukulele again so she could sing to the boys. He heard from up the street the water-like sounds of the ladies' party, and off through the trees where the big boys were playing, sounds of the ball being knocked out—gay and removed as birdsong. But the tick-tock was sharper and clearer than all he could hear just now in the world, and at moments seemed to ring close, the way his own heartbeat rang against the bed he came out of.

His mother, had it been she in the vacant house, would have stopped those two Negroes straggling home with their unsold peas and made them come in off the street and do all that for her, and finish up in no time. But the sailor's mother was doing her work alone. She wanted things to suit herself, nobody else would have been able to please her; and she was taking her own sweet time. She was building a bonfire of her own in the piano and would set off the dynamite when she was ready and not before.

Loch knew from her actions that the contrivance down in the wires—the piano front had been taken away—was a kind of nest. She was building it like a thieving bird, weaving in every little scrap that she could find around her. He saw in two places the mustached face of Mr. Drewsie Carmichael, his father's candidate for mayor—she found the circulars in the door. The litter on his bed, the Octagon Soap coupons, would have pleased her at that moment, and he would have turned them over to her.

Then Loch almost gave a yell; pride filled him, like a second yell, that he did not. Here down the street came Old Man Moody, the marshal, and Mr. Fatty Bowles with him. They had taken the day off to go fishing in Moon Lake and came carrying their old fishing canes but no fish. Their pants and shoes were heavy with mud. They were cronies of old Mr. Holifield and often came to wake him up, this time of day, and hound him off to the gin.

Loch skinned the cat over the limb and waited head down as they came tramping, sure enough, across the yard. In his special vision he saw that they could easily be lying on their backs in the blue sky and waving their legs pleasantly around, having nothing to do with law and order.

Old Man Moody and Mr. Fatty Bowles divided at the pecan stump, telling a joke, joined, said "Bread and butter," and then clogged up the steps. The curtain at the front window flapped signaling in their faces. They looked at each other anew. Their bodies and their faces grew smooth as fishes. They floated around the porch and flattened like fishes to nose at the window. There were round muddy spots on the seats of their pants; they squatted.

Well, there it is, thought Loch—the houseful. Two upstairs, one downstairs, and the two on the porch. And on the piano sat the ticking machine. . . . Directly below Loch a spotted thrush walked noisily in the weeds, pointing her beak ahead of her straight as a gun, just as busy in the world as people.

He held his own right hand ever so still as the old woman, unsteady as the Christmas angel in Mrs. McGillicuddy's fourth-grade pageant, came forward with a lighted candle in her hand. It was a kitchen tallow candle; she must have taken it out of Mr. Holifield's boxful against all the times the lights went out in Morgana. She came so slowly and held the candle so high that he could have popped it with a pea-shooter from where he was. Her hair, he saw, was cropped and white and lighted up all around. From the swaying, farthest length of a branch that would hold his weight, he could see how bright her big eyes were under their black circling brows, and how seldom they blinked. They were owl eyes.

She bent over, painfully, he felt, and laid the candle in the paper nest she had built in the piano. He too drew his breath in, protecting the flame, and as she pulled her aching hand back he pulled his. The newspaper caught, it was ablaze, and the old woman threw in the candle. Hands to thighs, she raised up, her work done.

Flames arrowed out so noiselessly. They ran down the streamers of paper, as double-quick as freshets from a loud gully-washer of rain. The room was criss-crossed with quick, dying yellow fire, there were pinwheels falling and fading from the ceiling. And up above, on the other side of the ceiling, they, the first two, were as still as mice.

The law still squatted. Mr. Fatty's and Old Man Moody's necks stretched sideways, the fat and the thin. Loch could have dropped a caterpillar down onto either of their heads, which rubbed together like mother's and child's.

"So help me. She *done* it," Mr. Fatty Bowles said in a natural voice. He lifted his arm, that had been hugging Old Man Moody's shoulders, and transferred to his own back pocket a slap that would have cracked Old Man Moody's bones. "Bless her heart! She done it before our eyes. What would you have bet?"

"Not a thing," said Old Man Moody. "Watch. If it catches them old dried-out squares of matting, Booney Holifield's going to feel a little warm ere long."

"Booney! Why, I done forgot him!"

Old Man Moody laughed explosively with shut lips.

"Wouldn't you say it's done caught now," said Mr. Fatty, pointing into the room with his old fishing knife.

"The house is on fire!" Loch cried at the top of his voice. He was riding his limb up and down and shaking the leaves.

Old Man Moody and Mr. Fatty might have heard, for, a little as if they were insulted, they raised up, moved their fishing poles along, and deliberately chose the dining room window instead of the parlor window to get to work on.

They lifted the screen out, and Mr. Fatty accidentally stepped through it. They inched the sash up with a sound that made them draw high their muck-coated heels. They could go in now: they opened their mouths and guffawed silently. They were so used to showing off, they almost called up Morgana then and there.

Mr. Fatty Bowles started to squeeze himself over the sill into the room, but Old Man Moody was ready for that, pulled him back by the suspenders, and went first. He leap-frogged it. Inside, they both let go a holler.

"Look out! You're caught in the act!"

In the parlor, the old lady backed herself into the blind corner.

Old Man Moody and Mr. Fatty made a preliminary run around the dining room table to warm up, and then charged the parlor. They trod down the barrier of sparky matting and stomped in. They boxed at the smoke, hit each other, and ran to put up the window. Then Loch heard their well-known coughs and the creep and crack of fire inside the room. The smoke mostly stayed inside, contained and still.

Loch skinned the cat again. Here came somebody else. It was a fine day! Presently he thought he knew the golden Panama hat, and the elastic spareness of the man under it. He used to live in that vacant house and had at that time promised to bring Loch a talking bird, one that could say "Rabbits!" He had left and never returned. After all the years, Loch still wanted a bird like that. It was to his taste today.

"Nobody lives there now!" Loch called out of the leaves in an appropriate voice, for Mr. Voight turned in just like home at the vacant house. "If you go in, you'll blow up."

There was no talking bird on his shoulder yet. It was a long time ago that Mr. Voight had promised it. (And how often, Loch thought now with great surprise, he had remembered and cherished the promise!)

Mr. Voight shook his head rapidly as though a far-away voice from the leaves bothered him only for a moment. He ran up the steps with a sound like a green stick along a fence. He, though, instead of running into the flapping barrier over the door, drifted around the porch to the side and leisurely took a look through the window. Everything made his shout alarming.

"Will you please tell me why you're trespassing here?"

"So help me!" said Mr. Fatty Bowles, who was looking right at him, holding a burning hat.

71

Old Man Moody only said, "*Good* evening. Now I don't speak to you."

"Answer me! Trespassing, are you?"

"Whoa. Your house is afire."

"If my house is afire, then where's my folks gone?"

"Oh, *'tain't* your house no more, I forgot. It's Miss Francine Murphy's house. You're late, Captain."

"What antics are these? Get out of my house. Put that fire out behind you. Tell me where they went. Never mind, I know where they went. All right, burn it down, who's to stop you?"

He slapped his hands on the boarding of the house, fanfare like, and must have glared at them between, at the window. He had inserted himself between Loch and what happened, and to tell the truth he made one too many.

Old Man Moody and Mr. Fatty, exchanging murderous looks, ran hopping about the parlor, clapping their hats at the skittering flames, working in a team mad at itself, the way two people try to head off chickens in a yard. They jumped up and knocked at the same flame. They kicked and rubbed under their feet a spark they found by themselves, sometimes imaginary. Maybe because they'd let the fire almost go out, or because Mr. Voight had come to criticize, they pretended this fire was bigger than it had ever been. They bit their underlips tightly as old people do in carrying out acts of rudeness. They didn't speak.

Mr. Voight shook all over. He was laughing, Loch discovered. Now he watched the room like a show. "That's it! That's it!" he said.

Old Man Moody and Mr. Bowles together beat out the fire in the piano, fighting over it hard, banging and twanging the strings. Old Man Moody, no matter how his fun had been spoiled, enjoyed jumping up and down on the fierce-burning magnolia leaves. So they put the fire out, every spark, even the matting, which twinkled all over time and again before it went out for good. When a little tongue of flame started up for the last time, they quenched it together; and with a whistle and one more stamp each, they dared it, and it stayed out.

"That's it, boys," said Mr. Voight.

Then the old woman came out of the blind corner. "Now who's this?" cried Mr. Voight. In the center of the room she stopped. Without the law to stand over her, she might have clasped her empty hands and turned herself this way and that. But she did not; she was more desperate still. Loch hollered out again, riding the tree, his branch in both fists.

"Why don't you step on in, Captain?" called Mr. Fatty Bowles, and he beckoned the old lady to him.

"Down to business here. Now I'd appreciate knowing why you done this, lady," Old Man Moody said, rubbing his eyes and rimming them with black. "Putting folks to all this trouble. Now what you got against us?"

"Cat's got her tongue," said Mr. Fatty.

"I'm an old man. But you're an old woman. *I* don't know why you done it. Unless of course it was for pure lack of good sense."

"Where you come from?" asked Mr. Fatty in his little tenor voice.

"You clowns."

Mr. Voight, who said that, now went lightly as a dragonfly around the porch and entered the house by the front door: it was not locked. He might have been waiting until all the beating about had been done by others—clowns—or perhaps he thought he was so valuable that he could burn up in too big a hurry.

Loch saw him step, with rather a flare, through the beads at the hall door and come into the parlor. He gazed serenely about the walls, pausing for a moment first, as though something had happened to them not that very hour but a long time ago. He was there and not there, for he alone was not at his wit's end. He went picking his feet carefully among the frills and flakes of burned paper, and wrinkled up his sharp nose; not from the smell, it seemed, but from wider, dissolving things. Now he stood at the window. His eyes rolled. Would he foam at the mouth? He did once. If he did not, Loch might not be sure about him; he remembered Mr. Voight best as foaming.

"Do you place her, Captain?" asked Old Man Moody in a cautious voice. "Who's this here firebug? You been places."

Mr. Voight was strolling about the room, and taking the poker he poked among the ashes. He picked up a seashell. The old lady advanced on him and he put it back, and as he came up he took off his hat. It looked more than polite. There close to the old lady's face he cocked his head, but she looked through him, a long way through Mr. Voight. She could have been a lady on an opposite cliff, far away, out of eye range and earshot, but about to fall.

The tick-tock was very loud then. Just as Mr. Fatty had forgotten Mr. Booney Holifield, Loch had forgotten the dynamite. Now he could go back to expecting a blast. The fire had had a hard time, but fire could manage to connect itself with an everlasting little mechanism that could pound like that, right along, right in the room.

("Do you hear something, Mr. Moody?" Loch could cry out right now. "Mr. Voight, listen."—"All right, say—do you want your bird this minute?" might be the reply. "We'll call everything off.")

"Man, what's that?" asked Mr. Fatty Bowles, and "Fatty boy, do you hear something ugly?" Old Man Moody asked at the same instant. At last they cocked their ears at the ticking that had been there in the room with them all this time. They looked at each other and then with hunched shoulders paraded around looking for the source of it.

"It's a rattlesnake! No, it ain't! But it's close," said Mr. Fatty.

They looked high and low all over the room but they couldn't see it right in front of their eyes and up just a little, on top of the piano. That was honestly not a fair place, not where most people would put a thing. They looked at each other harder and hurried faster, but all they did

was run on each other's heels and tip the chairs over. One of the chair
legs snapped like a chicken bone.

Mr. Voight only got in their way, since he did not move an inch. He
was still standing before the eyes of the sailor's mother, looking at her
with lips puckered. It could be indeed that he knew her from his
travels. He looked tired from these same travels now.

At last Old Man Moody, the smarter one of those two, spied what
they were looking for, the obelisk with its little moving part and its door
open. Once seen, that thing was so surely *it* that he merely pointed it
out to Mr. Fatty. Mr. Fatty tiptoed over and picked the obelisk up and
set it down again quickly. So Old Man Moody stumped over and picked
it up and held it up on the diagonal, posing, like a fisherman holding a
funny-looking fish to have come out of Moon Lake.

The old woman lifted her head and walked around Mr. Voight to Old
Man Moody. She reached up and took the ticking thing right out of his
hand, and he turned it loose agreeably; Old Man Moody seemed not
taken by surprise by women.

The old woman held her possession to her, drawn to her big gray
breast. Her eyesight returned from far to close by. Then she stood looking at the three people fixedly, as if she showed them her insides, her
live heart.

And then a little whir of her own voice: "See . . . See, Mr. MacLain."

Nothing blew up, but Mr. Voight (but she called him MacLain)
groaned.

"No, boys. I never saw her in my life," he said.

He walked stiffly out of the room. He walked out of the house
and cater-cornered across the yard toward the MacLain Road. As he
reached the road itself, he put his hat on, and then he did not look as
shabby, or as poor.

Loch clasped a leafy armful of the tree and sank his head in the
green cool.

"Let *me* see your play-pretty," Mr. Fatty Bowles was saying with his baby-smile. He took the obelisk away from the old woman, and with a sudden change on his face threw it with all his might out the open window. It came straight toward Loch, and fell into the weeds below him. And still it ticked.

"You could have been a little too quick there, Fatty boy," said Old Man Moody. "Flinging evidence."

"You ought to think about us. Listen and you'll hear it blow up. I'd rather have it blow up your wife's chickens."

"Well, I wouldn't."

And while they talked, the poor old woman tried it again. She was down on her knees cradling the lump of candle and the next moment had it lighted. She rose up, agitated now, and went running about the room, holding the candle above her, evading the men each time they tried to head her off.

This time, the fire caught her own hair. The little short white frill turned to flame.

Old Man Moody was so quick that he caught her. He came up with a big old rag from somewhere, and ran after the old woman with it. They both ran extraordinarily fast. He had to make a jump. He brought the cloth down over her head from behind, grimacing, as if all people on earth had to do acts of shame, some time. He hit her covered-up head about with the flat of his hand.

Old Man Moody and Mr. Bowles brought the old woman between them out on the porch of the vacant house. She was quiet now, with the scorched black cloth covering her head; she herself held it on with both hands.

"Know what I'm going to have to do with you?" Old Man Moody was saying gently and conversationally, but she only stood there, all cov-

ered in wrinkled cloth with her little hands up, clawed, the way a
locust shell would be found clinging to that empty door in August.

"It don't signify nothing what your name is now, or what you intended, old woman," Mr. Bowles told her as he got the fishing canes.
"We know where you belong at, and that's Jackson."

"Come on ladylike. I'm sure you know how," Old Man Moody said.

She came along but she did not answer either man anything.

"Maybe she aimed mischief at King MacLain after all," said Mr.
Fatty Bowles. "She a she, ain't she?"

"That'll be enough out of you for the rest of the day," said Old Man
Moody.

Among the leaves, Loch watched them come down the walk and
head towards town. They went slowly, for the old woman took short,
hesitant steps. Where would they take her now? Not later, to Jackson,
but now? After they passed, he let go his hands and jumped out of the
tree. It made a good noise when he hit ground. He turned a forward and
a backward somersault and started walking on his hands around the
tree trunk. He made noises like a goat, and a bobwhite, like the silly
Moody chickens, and like a lion.

On his hands he circled the tree and the obelisk waited in the weeds,
upright. He stood up and looked at it. Its ticker was outside it.

He felt charmed like a bird, for the ticking stick went like a tail, a
tongue, a wand. He picked the box up in his hands.

"Now go on. Blow up."

When he examined it, he saw the beating stick to be a pendu-
lum that instead of hanging down stuck upwards. He touched it and
stopped it with his finger. He felt its pressure, and the weight of the
obelisk, which seemed about two pounds. He released the stick, and it
went on beating.

Then he turned a little key in the side of the box, and that controlled

He stood up and looked at it. Its ticker was outside it.

it. The stick stopped and he poked it into place within the box, and shut the door of the thing.

It might not be dynamite: especially since Mr. Fatty thought it was. What was it?

He opened his shirt and buttoned it in. He thought he might take it up to his room. It was this; not a bird that knew how to talk.

The sand pile was before him now. He planed away the hot top layer and sat down. He held still for a while, while nothing was ticking. Nothing but the crickets. Nothing but the train going through, ticking its two cars over the Big Black bridge.

IV

Cassie moved to the front window, where she could see Old Man Moody and Mr. Fatty Bowles carrying off the old woman. The old woman was half sick or dazed. She held on her head some nameless kitchen rag; she had no purse. In a gray housedress prophetic of an institution she was making her way along, about to be touched, prodded, any minute, but not worrying about it. She wore shoes without stockings—and she had such white, white ankles. When she saw the ankles, Cassie flung herself in full view at the window and gave a cry.

No head lifted. Cassie rushed out of her room, down the stairs and out the front door.

To Loch's amazement his sister Cassie came running barefooted down the front walk in her petticoat and in full awareness turned towards town, crying, "You can't take her! Miss Eckhart!"

She was too late for anybody to hear her, of course, but he creaked up out of the sand pile and ran out after her as if they had heard. He caught up with her and pulled at her petticoat. She turned, with her head still swimming high in the air, and cried softly, "Oh, Mother!"

They looked at each other.

"Crazy."

79

"Crazy yourself."

"Back yonder," said Loch presently, "I can show you how ripe the figs are." They withdrew as far as the tree. But it was only in time to see the sailor and Virgie Rainey run out, trying to escape by the back way. Virgie and the sailor saw them. Back into the house they ran, and then, in utter recklessness, out the front, the sailor first. The Morrisons had nowhere to go.

Old Man Moody's party was only now progressing again, for the old woman had fallen down and they had to hold her on her feet. Farther along, the ladies' Rook party was coming out of Miss Nell's with a pouring sound. The sailor faced both these ranks.

The marshal tagged him but he ran straight on into the wall of ladies, most of whom cried "Why, Kewpie Moffitt!"—an ancient nickname he had outgrown. He whirled about-face and ran the other way, and since he was carrying his blouse and was naked from the waist up, his collar stood out behind him like the lowest-hung wings. At the Carmichael corner, he tried east and took west, and ran into the shadows of the short-cut to the river, where he would just about meet with Mr. King MacLain, if he was not too late.

"Look at that!" Miss Billy Texas Spights called clearly. "I see you, Virgie Rainey!"

"Mother!" Cassie called, just as clearly. She and Loch found themselves out in front again.

The front door of the empty house fell to with a frail sound behind Virgie Rainey. A haze of the old smoke lifted unhurryingly over her, brushed and hid her for a moment like a gauzy cloud. She was coming right out, though, in a home-made dress of apricot voile, carrying a mesh bag on a chain. She ran down the steps and walked clicking her heels out to the sidewalk—always Virgie clicked her heels as if nothing had happened in the past or behind her, as if she were free, whatever else she might be. The ladies hushed, holding on to

their prizes and folded parasols. Virgie faced them as she turned towards town.

It was the hour, of course, for her to go to work. Once past the next
corner, she could drink a Coca-Cola and eat a box of cakes at Loomis's
drug store, as she did every evening for her supper; then she could
vanish inside the Bijou.

She passed Cassie and Loch, cutting them, and kept going and
caught up, as she had to, with the marshal, Fatty Bowles, and the old
woman.

"You're running the wrong way!" Miss Billy Texas Spights called
loudly. "Better run after that sailor boy!"

"Isn't he visiting the Flewellyns out in the country?" Miss Perdita
Mayo was pleading to everybody. "What ever became of his mother?
I'd forgotten all about him!"

Pinning Loch tightly by the arms in front of her, Cassie could only
think: we were spies too. And nobody else was surprised at anything—
it was only we two. People saw things like this as they saw Mr. Mac-
Lain come and go. They only hoped to place them, in their hour or
their street or the name of their mothers' people. Then Morgana could
hold them, and at last they were this and they were that. And when
ruin was predicted all along, even if people had forgotten it was on the
way, even if they mightn't have missed it if it hadn't appeared, still
they were never surprised when it came.

"She'll stop for Miss Eckhart," breathed Cassie.

Virgie went by. There was a meeting of glances between the teacher
and her old pupil, that Cassie knew. She could not be sure that Miss
Eckhart's eyes closed once in recall—they had looked so wide-open at
everything alike. The meeting amounted only to Virgie Rainey's passing by, in plain fact. She clicked by Miss Eckhart and she clicked
straight through the middle of the Rook party, without a word or the
pause of a moment.

Old Man Moody and Fatty Bowles, dirty, their faces shining like the fish they didn't catch, took advantage of the path Virgie cut through the ladies and walked Miss Eckhart, unprotesting, on. Then the ladies brought their ranks safely to, and Miss Billy Texas, suddenly beside herself, cried once more, "He went the *other* way, Virgie!"

"That's enough, Billy Texas," said Miss Lizzie Stark. "As if her mother didn't have enough on her, just burying her son."

The noise of tin pans being beaten came from the distance, then little children's and Negro nurses' cries, "Crazy! Crazy!"

Cassie turned on Loch, pulled him to her and shook him by the shoulders. He was wet as a dishrag. A row of those big salt-and-pepper-colored mosquitoes perched all along his forehead. "What were you doing out of your bed, anyway?" she asked in a matter-of-fact, scolding voice. Loch gave her a long, gratified look. "What have you got there inside your nighties, crazy?"

"None of your business."

"Give it to me."

"It's mine."

"It is not. Let go."

"You make me."

"All right, I know what it is."

"What is it? You do not."

"You can't have that."

"Get away from me."

"I'll tell Mama and Papa.—You hit me! You hit a girl where she's tender."

"Well, you know you can't have it."

"All right then—did you see Mr. MacLain? He's been gone since you were born."

"Why, sure," said Loch. "I saw Mr. MacLain."

82

"Oh, Loch, why don't you beat off those mosquitoes!" She wept. "Mother!" Even Loch flew from her, at once.

"Well, here I am," said her mother.

"Oh!" After a moment she raised her head to say, "And Mr. King MacLain was here, and now he's gone."

"Well. You've seen him before," said her mother after a moment, breaking from her. "That's no excuse for coming outdoors in your petticoat to cry."

"You knew it would be this way, you were with them!"

There was no answer then either, and Cassie trudged through the yard. Loch stood near the sand pile. His lips clamped down, he held his bulging nightie and regarded it. She ran him back under the tree and into the house by the back door.

"What orphan-lookin' children is these here?" said Louella. "Where yawl orphan come from? Yawl don't live here, yawl live at County Orphan. Gawn back."

Cassie pushed Loch through the kitchen and then pulled him to a stop in the back hall. It was their father coming home.

"What's going on here! The house is on fire, the MacLain house! I see smoke!"

They could see him coming up the front walk, waving the rolled-up *Bugle* he brought home every night.

"Holifield! Holifield!"

Mr. Holifield must have come to the window, for they heard, "Did I hear my name called?" and they sighed with foreboding.

"It's gone out, Wilbur," said their mother at the door.

"That house has been on fire *and* gone out, sir." Their father was speaking loudly as he did from the platform at election time. "You can read about it in tomorrow's *Bugle*."

"Come in, Wilbur."

They could see her finger tracing a little pattern on the screen door as she stood there in her party dress. "Cassie says King MacLain was here and gone. That's as interesting as twenty fires."

Cassie shivered.

"Maybe this will bestir Francine Murphy to take a step. *There's* a public guardian for you: Booney Holifield."

Cassie was glad her father kept on. If there was anything that unsettled him it was for people not to be on the inside what their outward semblances led you to suppose. "MacLain came to the wrong place this time. It might have caught *our* house: Booney Holifield!"

Their mother laughed. "That old monkey," she said. As far as she was concerned, the old man next door had just come alive, redeemed himself a little from being a Holifield.

The six-o'clock summer light shone just as usual on their father and mother meeting at the door.

"Come on."

Cassie and Loch running up the back stairs heard the sigh of the door and the old, muffled laugh that came between their parents at this moment. No matter what had happened, or had started to happen, around them, they could come in the house and laugh about the old thing. Theirs was a laugh that hinted of some small but interesting object, a thing even their deliberate father could find—something that might be seizable and holdable as well as findable, as ridiculous and forbidden to children, as alive, as a stray kitten or a rabbit.

The children kept on going up the steep dark backstairs, so close on each other they prodded and nudged each other, both punishing and petting.

"Get back in bed like you were never out," Cassie advised. "Pull the beggarlice off you."

"But I think Mother saw me," he said over his shoulder, going.

Cassie didn't answer.

She shivered and walked into her room. There was the scarf. It was
an old friend, part enemy. She brought it to her face, touched her lips
to it, breathed its smoky dye-smell, and passed it up her cheeks and
over her eyes. She pressed it against her forehead. She might have lost
it, might have run out with it . . . for she had visions of poor Miss
Eckhart wearing it away over her head; of Virgie waving it, brazenly, in
the air of the street; of too-knowing Jinny Love Stark asking, "Couldn't
you keep it?"

"Listen and I'll tell you what Miss Nell served at the party," Loch's
mother said softly, with little waits in her voice. She was just a glimmer
at the foot of his bed.

"Ma'am."

"An orange scooped out and filled with orange juice, with the top put
back on and decorated with icing leaves, a straw stuck in. A slice of
pineapple with a heap of candied sweet potatoes on it, and a little
handle of pastry. A cup made out of toast, filled with creamed chicken,
fairly warm. A sweet peach pickle with flower petals around it of differ-
ent-colored cream cheese. A swan made of a cream puff. He had whipped cream feathers, a pastry neck, green icing eyes. A pastry biscuit
the size of a marble with a little date filling." She sighed abruptly.

"Were you hungry, Mama?" he said.

It was not really to him that his mother would be talking, but it was
he who tenderly let her, as they watched and listened to the swallows
just at dark. It was always at this hour that she spoke in this voice—
not to him or to Cassie or Louella or to his father, or to the evening, but
to the wall, more nearly. She bent seriously over him and kissed him
hard, and swayed out of the room.

There was singing in the street. He saw Cassie, a lesser but similar
gleam, go past his door. The hay wagon was coming up the street to get
her. He heard the girls and boys hail her, and her greeting the same

as theirs, as if nothing had happened up until now, heard them pull
her up. Ran MacLain from MacLain Courthouse, or was it his brother
Eugene, always called to Mrs. Morrison, teasing, "Come on! You come
with us!" Did they really want to take her? He heard the wagon creak
away. They were singing and playing on their ukuleles, some song of
which he couldn't be sure.

Presently Loch lifted up and gazed through the same old leaves,
dark once more, and saw the vacant house looking the same as it ever
did. A cloud lighted anew, low in the deep sky, a single long wing. The
mystery he had felt like a golden and aimless bird had waited until now
to fly over. Until now, when all else had been driven out. His body
shook. Perhaps the fever would go now, and the chill come.

But Louella brought him his supper, and waited while he ate it, sitting quietly. She had made him chicken broth that sparkled like dia-
monds in the evening light, and then there would be the junket he
hated, turning to water under his tongue.

"Louella, I don't want junket tonight. Louella, listen. Do you hear a
thing ticking?"

"Hear it plain."

She took his tray and sat down again, and he lay on his back, looking upward. High in the sky the quarter moon was bright. "Reckon it's
going to blow up in the night? You can see it. Look on the washstand."
All by itself, of its own accord, it might let fly its little door and start
up. He thought he heard it now. Or was it his father's watch in the next
room, already laid on the dresser for the night?

"I 'spec' it will, Loch, if you wants it to," she said readily, and sat
on in the dark. She added, "Blow up? If it do, I'll wrang your neck.
Next time you scoot down that tree and come back draggin' sompm.
Listen that big bullfrog in the swamp, you want to listen to sompm
might blow up."

They looked at each other and neither wished to speak.

He listened, lying stretched and pointed in the four directions. His heart pumping the secret anticipation that parted his lips, he fell into space and floated. Even floating, he felt the pressure of his frown and heard his growling voice and the gnashing of his teeth. He dreamed close to the surface, and his dreams were filled with a color and a fury that the daytime that summer never held.

Later, in her moonlit bed, Cassie lay thinking. Her hair and the inner side of her arms still smelled of hay; she tasted the sweet summer dryness in her mouth. In the distances of her mind the wagon still rocked, rocking its young girls' burden, the teasing anxiety, the singing, the moon and stars and the moving roof of leaves, Moon Lake brimming and the boat on it, the smiling drowse of boys, and the way she herself had let nobody touch even her hand. And she thought back to the sailor beginning to run down the street, as strange a sight with his clothes partly missing as a mer-man from the lake, and around again to Miss Eckhart and Virgie coming together on the deadquiet sidewalk. What she was certain of was the distance those two had gone, as if all along they had been making a trip (which the sailor was only starting). It had changed them. They were deliberately terrible. They looked at each other and neither wished to speak. They did not even horrify each other. No one could touch them now, either.

Danke schoen . . . That much was out in the open. Gratitude—like rescue—was simply no more. It was not only past; it was outworn and cast away. Both Miss Eckhart and Virgie Rainey were human beings terribly at large, roaming on the face of the earth. And there were others of them—human beings, roaming, like lost beasts.

Into her head flowed the whole of the poem she had found in that book. It ran perfectly through her head, vanishing as it went, one line yielding to the next, like a torch race. All of it passed through her head, through her body. She slept, but sat up in bed once and said aloud, "*'Because a fire was in my head.'*" Then she fell back unresisting. She did not see except in dreams that a face looked in; that it was the grave, unappeased, and radiant face, once more and always, the face that was in the poem.

MOONLAKE

F ROM THE BEGINNING HIS MAR-
tyred presence seriously affected them. They had a disquieting famil-
iarity with it, hearing the spit of his despising that went into his bugle.
At times they could hardly recognize what he thought he was playing.
Loch Morrison, Boy Scout and Life Saver, was under the ordeal of a
week's camp on Moon Lake with girls.

Half the girls were county orphans, wished on them by Mr. Nesbitt
and the Men's Bible Class after Billy Sunday's visit to town; but all
girls, orphans and Morgana girls alike, were the same thing to Loch;
maybe he threw in the two councilors too. He was hating every day of
the seven. He hardly spoke; he never spoke first. Sometimes he swung
in the trees; Nina Carmichael in particular would hear him crashing in
the foliage somewhere when she was lying rigid in siesta.

While they were in the lake, for the dip or the five-o'clock swimming
period in the afternoon, he stood against a tree with his arms folded,
jacked up one-legged, sitting on his heel, as absolutely tolerant as an
old fellow waiting for the store to open, being held up by the wall.
Waiting for the girls to get out, he gazed upon some undisturbed part of
the water. He despised their predicaments, most of all their not being
able to swim. Sometimes he would take aim and from his right cheek
shoot an imaginary gun at something far out, where they never were.
Then he resumed his pose. He had been roped into this by his mother.

He blew his horn into their presence—trees' and girls'—and then watched the Dip.

At the hours too hot for girls he used Moon Lake. He dived high off the crosspiece nailed up in the big oak, where the American Legion dived. He went through the air rocking and jerking like an engine, splashed in, climbed out, spat, climbed up again, dived off. He wore a long bathing suit which stretched longer from Monday to Tuesday and from Tuesday to Wednesday and so on, yawning at the armholes toward infinity, and it looked black and formal as a minstrel suit as he stood skinny against the clouds as on a stage.

He came and got his food and turned his back and ate it all alone like a dog and lived in a tent by himself, apart like the cook, and dived alone when the lake was clear of girls. That way, he seemed able to bear it; that would be his life. In early evening, in moonlight sings, the Boy Scout and Life Saver kept far away. They would sing "When all the little ships come sailing home," and he would be roaming off; they could tell about where he was. He played taps for them, invisibly then, and so beautifully they wept together, whole tentfuls some nights. Off with the whip-poor-wills and the coons and the owls and the little bob-whites—down where it all sloped away, he had pitched his tent, and slept there. Then at reveille, how he would spit into that cornet.

Reveille was his. He harangued the woods when the little minnows were trembling and running wizardlike in the water's edge. And how lovely and altered the trees were then, weighted with dew, leaning on one another's shoulders and smelling like big wet flowers. He blew his horn into their presence—trees' and girls'—and then watched the Dip.

"Good morning, Mr. Dip, Dip, Dip, with your water just as cold as ice!" sang Mrs. Gruenwald hoarsely. She took them for the dip, for Miss Moody said she couldn't, simply couldn't.

The orphans usually hung to the rear, and every other moment stood swayback with knees locked, the shoulders of their wash dresses ironed flat and stuck in peaks, and stared. For swimming they owned

95

no bathing suits and went in in their underbodies. Even in the water they would stand swayback, each with a fist in front of her over the rope, looking over the flat surface as over the top of a tall mountain none of them could ever get over. Even at this hour of the day, they seemed to be expecting little tasks, something more immediate—little tasks that were never given out.

Mrs. Gruenwald was from the North and said "dup." "Good morning, Mr. Dup, Dup, Dup, with your water just as cold as ice!" sang Mrs. Gruenwald, fatly capering and leading them all in a singing, petering-out string down to the lake. She did a sort of little rocking dance in her exhortation, broad in her bathrobe. From the tail end of the line she looked like a Shredded Wheat Biscuit box rocking on its corners.

Nina Carmichael thought, There is nobody and nothing named Mr. Dip, it is not a good morning until you have had coffee, and the water is the temperature of a just-cooling biscuit, thank Goodness. I hate this little parade of us girls, Nina thought, trotting fiercely in the center of it. It ruins the woods, all right. "Gee, we think you're mighty nice," they sang to Mr. Dip, while the Boy Scout, waiting at the lake, watched them go in.

"Watch out for mosquitoes," they called to one another, lyrically because warning wasn't any use anyway, as they walked out of their kimonos and dropped them like the petals of one big scattered flower on the bank behind them, and exposing themselves felt in a hundred places at once the little pangs. The orphans ripped their dresses off over their heads and stood in their underbodies. Busily they hung and piled their dresses on a cedar branch, obeying one of their own number, like a whole flock of ferocious little birds with pale topknots building themselves a nest. The orphan named Easter appeared in charge. She handed her dress wrong-side-out to a friend, who turned it and

96

hung it up for her, and waited standing very still, her little fingers locked.

"Let's let the orphans go in the water first and get the snakes stirred up, Mrs. Gruenwald," Jinny Love Stark suggested first off, in the cheerful voice she adopted toward grown people. "Then they'll be chased away by the time *we* go in."

That made the orphans scatter in their pantie-waists, outwards from Easter; the little gauzes of gnats they ran through made them beat their hands at the air. They ran back together again, to Easter, and stood excitedly, almost hopping.

"I think we'll all go in in one big bunch," Mrs. Gruenwald said. Jinny Love lamented and beat against Mrs. Gruenwald, Mrs. Gruenwald's solid, rope-draped stomach all but returning her blows. "All take hands—march! Into the water! *Don't* let the stobs and cypress roots break your legs! *Do* your best! Kick! Stay on top if you can and hold the rope if necessary!"

Mrs. Gruenwald abruptly walked away from Jinny Love, out of the bathrobe, and entered the lake with a vast displacing. She left them on the bank with her Yankee advice.

The Morgana girls might never have gone in if the orphans hadn't balked. Easter came to a dead stop at Moon Lake and looked at it squinting as though it floated really on the Moon. And mightn't it be on the Moon?—it was a strange place, Nina thought, unlikely—and three miles from Morgana, Mississippi, all the time. The Morgana girls pulled the orphans' hands and dragged them in, or pushed suddenly from behind, and finally the orphans took hold of one another and waded forward in a body, singing "Good Morning" with their stiff, chiplike lips. None of them could or would swim, ever, and they just stood waist-deep and waited for the dip to be over. A few of them reached out and caught the struggling Morgana girls by the legs as they splashed from one barky post to another, to see how hard it really was to stay up.

"Mrs. Gruenwald, look, they want to drown us."

But Mrs. Gruenwald all this time was rising and sinking like a whale, she was in a sea of her own waves and perhaps of self-generated cold, out in the middle of the lake. She cared little that Morgana girls who learned to swim were getting a dollar from home. She had deserted them, no, she had never really been with them. Not only orphans had she deserted. In the water she kept so much to the profile that her single pushing-out eyeball looked like a little bottle of something. It was said she believed in evolution.

While the Boy Scout in the rosy light under the green trees twirled his horn so that it glittered and ran a puzzle in the sun, and emptied the spit out of it, he yawned, snappingly—as if he would bite the day, as quickly as Easter had bitten Deacon Nesbitt's hand on Opening Day.

"Gee, we think you're mighty nice," they sang to Mr. Dip, gasping, pounding their legs in him. If they let their feet go down, the invisible bottom of the lake felt like soft, knee-deep fur. The sharp hard knobs came up where least expected. The Morgana girls of course wore bathing slippers, and the mud loved to suck them off. The alligators had been beaten out of this lake, but it was said that water snakes—pilots—were swimming here and there; they would bite you but not kill you; and one cottonmouth moccasin was still getting away from the Negroes—if the Negroes were still going after him; he would kill you. These were the chances of getting sucked under, of being bitten, and of dying three miles away from home.

The brown water cutting her off at the chest, Easter looked directly before her, wide awake, unsmiling. Before she could hold a stare like that, she would have had to swallow something big—so Nina felt. It would have been something so big that it didn't matter to her what the inside of a snake's mouth was lined with. At the other end of her gaze the life saver grew almost insignificant. Her gaze moved like a little switch or wand, and the life saver scratched himself with his bugle, raked himself, as if that eased him. Yet the flick of a blue-bottle fly made Easter jump.

They swam and held to the rope, hungry and waiting. But they had to keep waiting till Loch Morrison blew his horn before they could come out of Moon Lake. Mrs. Gruenwald, who capered before breakfast, believed in evolution, and put her face in the water, was quarter of a mile out. If she said anything, they couldn't hear her for the frogs.

II

Nina and Jinny Love, with the soles of their feet shocked from the walk, found Easter ahead of them down at the spring.

For the orphans, from the first, sniffed out the way to the spring by themselves, and they could get there without stops to hold up their feet and pull out thorns and stickers, and could run through the sandy bottoms and never look down where they were going, and could grab hold with their toes on the sharp rutted path up the pine ridge and down. They clearly could never get enough of skimming over the silk-slick needles and setting prints of their feet in the bed of the spring to see them dissolve away under their eyes. What was it to them if the spring was muddied by the time Jinny Love Stark got there?

The one named Easter could fall flat as a boy, elbows cocked, and drink from the cup of her hand with her face in the spring. Jinny Love prodded Nina, and while they looked on Easter's drawers, Nina was opening the drinking cup she had brought with her, then collapsing it, feeling like a lady with a fan. That way, she was going over a thought, a fact: Half the people out here with me are orphans. Orphans. Orphans. She yearned for her heart to twist. But it didn't, not in time. Easter was

99

through drinking—wiping her mouth and flinging her hand as if to break the bones, to get rid of the drops, and it was Nina's turn with her drinking cup.

Nina stood and bent over from the waist. Calmly, she held her cup in the spring and watched it fill. They could all see how it spangled like a cold star in the curling water. The water tasted the silver cool of the rim it went over running to her lips, and at moments the cup gave her teeth a pang. Nina heard her own throat swallowing. She paused and threw a smile about her. After she had drunk she wiped the cup on her tie and collapsed it, and put the little top on, and its ring over her finger. With that, Easter, one arm tilted, charged against the green bank and mounted it. Nina felt her surveying the spring and all from above. Jinny Love was down drinking like a chicken, kissing the water only.

Easter was dominant among the orphans. It was not that she was so bad. The one called Geneva stole, for example, but Easter was dominant for what she was in herself—for the way she held still, sometimes. All orphans were at once wondering and stoic—at one moment loving everything too much, the next folding back from it, tightly as hard green buds growing in the wrong direction, closing as they go. But it was as if Easter signaled them. Now she just stood up there, watching the spring, with the name Easter—tacky name, as Jinny Love Stark was the first to say. She was medium size, but her hair seemed to fly up at the temples, being cropped and wiry, and this crest made her nearly as tall as Jinny Love Stark. The rest of the orphans had hair paler than their tanned foreheads—straight and tow, the greenish yellow of cornsilk that dimmed black at the roots and shadows, with burnt-out-looking bangs like young boys' and old men's hair; that was from picking in the fields. Easter's hair was a withstanding gold. Around the back of her neck beneath the hair was a dark band on her skin like the mark a gold bracelet leaves on the arm. It came to the Morgana girls with a feeling of elation: the ring was pure dirt. They liked to look at it, or to remember, too late, what it was—as now, when Easter had already lain down for a drink and left the spring. They liked to walk behind her and see her back, which seemed spectacular from crested gold head to hard, tough heel. Mr. Nesbitt, from the Bible Class, took Easter by the wrist and turned her around to him and looked just as hard at her front. She had started her breasts. What Easter did was to bite his right hand, his collection hand. It was wonderful to have with them someone dangerous but not, so far, or provenly, bad. When Nina's little lead-mold umbrella, the size of a clover, a Crackerjack prize, was stolen the first night of camp, that was Geneva, Easter's friend.

Jinny Love, after wiping her face with a hand-made handkerchief, pulled out a deck of cards she had secretly brought in her middy pocket. She dropped them down, bright blue, on a sandy place by the spring. "Let's play cassino. Do they call you *Easter?*"

Down Easter jumped, from the height of the bank. She came back to them. "Cassino, what's that?"

"All right, what do *you* want to play?"

"All right, I'll play you mumblety-peg."

"I don't know how you play that!" cried Nina.

"Who would ever want to know?" asked Jinny Love, closing the circle.

Easter flipped out a jack-knife and with her sawed fingernail shot out three blades.

"Do you carry that in the orphan asylum?" Jinny Love asked with some respect.

Easter dropped to her scarred and coral-colored knees. They saw the dirt. "Get down if you want to play me mumblety-peg," was all she said, "and watch out for your hands and faces."

They huddled down on the piney sand. The vivid, hurrying ants were everywhere. To the squinted eye they looked like angry, orange ponies as they rode the pine needles. There was Geneva, skirting behind a tree, but she never came close or tried to get in the game. She pretended to be catching doodlebugs. The knife leaped and quivered in the sandy arena smoothed by Easter's hand.

"I may not know how to play, but I bet I win," Jinny Love said.

Easter's eyes, lifting up, were neither brown nor green nor cat; they had something of metal, flat ancient metal, so that you could not see into them. Nina's grandfather had possessed a box of coins from Greece and Rome. Easter's eyes could have come from Greece or Rome that day. Jinny Love stopped short of apprehending this, and only took care to watch herself when Easter pitched the knife. The color in Easter's eyes could have been found somewhere, away—away, under lost leaves—strange as the painted color of the ants. Instead of round black holes in the center of her eyes, there might have been women's heads, ancient.

Easter, who had played so often, won. She nodded and accepted Jinny Love's barrette and from Nina a blue jay feather which she transferred to her own ear.

"I wouldn't be surprised if you cheated, and don't know what you had to lose if you lost," said Jinny Love thoughtfully but with an admiration almost fantastic in her.

Victory with a remark attached did not crush Easter at all, or she scarcely listened. Her indifference made Nina fall back and listen to the spring running with an endless sound and see how the July light like purple and yellow birds kept flickering under the trees when the wind blew. Easter turned her head and the new feather on her head shone changeably. A black funnel of bees passed through the air, throwing a funneled shadow, like a visitor from nowhere, another planet.

"We have to play again to see whose the drinking cup will be," Easter said, swaying forward on her knees.

Nina jumped to her feet and did a cartwheel. Against the spinning green and blue her heart pounded as heavily as she touched lightly.

"You ruined the game," Jinny Love informed Easter. "You don't know Nina." She gathered up her cards. "You'd think it was made of fourteen-carat gold, and didn't come out of the pocket of an old suitcase, that cup."

"I'm sorry," said Nina sincerely.

As the three were winding around the lake, a bird flying above the opposite shore kept uttering a cry and then diving deep, plunging into the trees there, and soaring to cry again.

"Hear him?" one of the Negroes said, fishing on the bank; it was Elberta's sister Twosie, who spoke as if a long, long conversation had been going on, into which she would intrude only the mildest words. "Know why? Know why, in de sky, he say 'Spirit? Spirit?' And den he dive *boom* and say 'GHOST'?"

"Why does he?" said Jinny Love, in a voice of objection.

"Yawl knows. *I* don't know," said Twosie, in her little high, helpless voice, and she shut her eyes. They couldn't seem to get on by her. On fine days there is danger of some sad meeting, the positive danger of it. "*I* don't know what he say dat for." Twosie spoke pitifully, as though accused. She sighed. "Yawl sho ain't got yo' eyes opem good, yawl. Yawl don't know what's out here in woods wid you."

"Well, what?"

'Yawl walk right by mans wid great big gun, could jump out at yawl. Yawl don't eem smellim."

"You mean Mr. Holifield? That's a flashlight he's got." Nina looked at Jinny Love for confirmation. Mr. Holifield was their handy man, or rather simply "the man to be sure and have around the camp." He could be found by beating for a long time on the porch of the American Legion boat house—he slept heavily. "He hasn't got a gun to jump out with."

"I know who you mean. I hear those boys. Just some big boys, like the MacLain twins or somebody, and who cares about them?" Jinny Love, with her switch, indented the thick mat of hair on Twosie's head and prodded and stirred it gently. She pretended to fish in Twosie's woolly head. "Why ain't *you* scared, then?"

"I is."

Twosie's eyelids fluttered. Already she seemed to be fishing in her night's sleep. While they gazed at her crouched, devoted figure, from which the long pole hung, all their passions flew home again and went huddled and soft to roost.

Back at the camp, Jinny Love told Miss Moody about the great big jack-knife. Easter gave it up.

"I didn't mean you couldn't *drink* out of my cup," Nina said, waiting for her. "Only you have to hold it carefully, it leaks. It's engraved."

Easter wouldn't even try it, though Nina dangled it on its ring right under her eyes. She didn't say anything, not even "It's pretty." Was she even thinking of it? Or if not, what did she think about?

"Sometimes orphans act like deaf-and-dumbs," said Jinny Love.

III

"Nina!" Jinny Love whispered across the tent, during siesta. "What do you think you're reading?"

Nina closed *The Re-Creation of Brian Kent*. Jinny Love was already coming directly across the almost-touching cots to Nina's, walking on her knees and bearing down over Gertrude, Etoile, and now Geneva.

With Jinny Love upon her, Geneva sighed. Her sleeping face looked as if she didn't want to. She slept as she swam, in her pantie-waist, she was in running position and her ribs went up and down frantically—a little box in her chest that expanded and shut without a second's rest between. Her cheek was pearly with afternoon moisture and her kitten-like teeth pearlier still. As Jinny Love hid her and went over, Nina seemed to see her still; even her vaccination mark looked too big for her.

Nobody woke up from being walked over, but after Jinny Love had fallen in bed with Nina, Easter gave a belated, dreaming sound. She had not even been in the line of march; she slept on the cot by the door, curved shell-like, both arms forward over her head. It was an inward sound she gave—now it came again—of such wholehearted and fateful concurrence with the thing dreamed, that Nina and Jinny Love took hands and made wry faces at each other.

Beyond Easter's cot the corona of afternoon flared and lifted in an intensity that came through the eyelids. There was nothing but light out there. True, the black Negroes inhabited it. Elberta moved slowly through it, as if she rocked a baby with her hips, carrying a bucket of scraps to throw in the lake—to get hail Columbia for it later. Her straw hat spiraled rings of orange and violet, like a top. Far, far down a vista of intolerable light, a tiny daub of black cotton, Twosie had stationed herself at the edge of things, and slept and fished.

Eventually there was Exum wandering with his fish pole—he could dance on a dime, Elberta said, he used to work for a blind man. Exum was smart for twelve years old; too smart. He found that hat he wore— not a sign of the owner. He had a hat like new, filled out a little with peanut shells inside the band to correct the size, and he like a little black peanut in it. It stood up and away from his head all around, and seemed only following him—on runners, perhaps, like those cartridges for change in Spights' store.

Easter's sighs and her prolonged or half-uttered words now filled the tent, just as the heat filled it. Her words fell in threes, Nina observed, like the mourning-dove's call in the woods.

Nina and Jinny Love lay speechless, doubling for themselves the already strong odor of Sweet Dreams Mosquito Oil, in a trance of endurance through the hour's siesta. Entwined, they stared—orphan-like themselves—past Easter's cot and through the tent opening as down a long telescope turned on an incandescent star, and saw the spiral of Elberta's hat return, and saw Exum jump over a stick and on the other side do a little dance in a puff of dust. They could hear the intermittent crash, splash of Loch Morrison using their lake, and Easter's voice calling again in her sleep, her unintelligible words.

But however Nina and Jinny Love made faces at they knew not what, Easter concurred; she thoroughly agreed.

The bugle blew for swimming. Geneva jumped so hard she fell off her cot. Nina and Jinny Love were indented with each other, like pressed leaves, and jumped free. When Easter, who had to be shaken, sat up drugged and stupid on her cot, Nina ran over to her.

"Listen. Wake up. Look, you can go in in my bathing shoes today."

She felt her eyes glaze with this plan of kindness as she stretched out her limp red shoes that hung down like bananas under Easter's gaze. But Easter dropped back on the cot and stretched her legs.

"Never mind your shoes. I don't have to go in the lake if I don't want to."

"You do. I never heard of that. Who picked you out? You do," they said, all gathering.

"You make me."

Easter yawned. She fluttered her eyes and rolled them back—she loved doing that. Miss Moody passed by and beamed in at them hovered around Easter's passive and mutinous form. All along she'd been afraid of some challenge to her counselorship, from the way she hurried by now, almost too daintily.

"Well, *I* know," Jinny Love said, sidling up. "I know as much as you know, Easter." She made a chant, which drove her hopping around the tent pole in an Indian step. "You don't have to go, if you don't want to go. And if it ain't so, you still don't have to go, if you don't want to go." She kissed her hand to them.

Easter was silent—but if she groaned when she waked, she'd only be imitating herself.

Jinny Love pulled on her bathing cap, which gave way and came down over her eyes. Even in blindness, she cried, "So you needn't think you're the only one, Easter, not always. What do you say to that?"

"I should worry, I should cry," said Easter, lying still, spread-eagled.

"Let's us run away from basket weaving," Jinny Love said in Nina's ear, a little later in the week.

"Just as soon."

"Grand. They'll think we're drowned."

They went out the back end of the tent, barefooted; their feet were as tough as anybody's by this time. Down in the hammock, Miss Moody was reading *The Re-Creation of Brian Kent* now. (Nobody knew whose book that was, it has been found here, the covers curled up like side combs. Perhaps anybody at Moon Lake who tried to read it felt cheated by the title, as applying to camp life, as Nina did, and laid it down for the next person.) Cat, the cook's cat, was sunning on a post and when they approached jumped to the ground like something poured out of a bottle, and went with them, in front.

They trudged down the slope past Loch Morrison's tent and took the track into the swamp. There they moved single file between two walls; by lifting their arms they could have touched one or the other pressing side of the swamp. Their toes exploded the dust that felt like the powder clerks pump into new kid gloves, as Jinny Love said twice. They were eye to eye with the finger-shaped leaves of the castor bean plants, put out like those gypsy hands that part the curtains at the back of rolling wagons, and wrinkled and coated over like the fortune-teller's face.

Mosquitoes struck at them; Sweet Dreams didn't last. The whining lifted like a voice, saying "I don't want . . ." At the girls' shoulders

107

Queen Anne's lace and elderberry and blackberry thickets, loaded heavily with flower and fruit and smelling with the melony smell of snake, overhung the ditch to touch them. The ditches had dried green or blue bottoms, cracked and glazed—like a dropped vase. "I hope we don't meet any boogerman," Jinny Love said cheerfully.

Sweet bay and cypress and sweetgum and live oak and swamp maple closing tight made the wall dense, and yet there was somewhere still for the other wall of vine; it gathered itself on the ground and stacked and tilted itself in the trees; and like a table in the tree the mistletoe hung up there black in the zenith. Buzzards floated from one side of the swamp to the other, as if choice existed for them—raggedly crossing the sky and shadowing the track, and shouldering one another on the solitary limb of a moon-white sycamore. Closer to the ear than lips could begin words came the swamp sounds—closer to the ear and nearer to the dreaming mind. They were a song of hilarity to Jinny Love, who began to skip. Periods of silence seemed hoarse, or the suffering from hoarseness, otherwise inexplicable, as though the world could stop. Cat was stalking something at the black edge of the ditch. The briars didn't trouble Cat at all, it was they that seemed to give way beneath that long, boatlike belly.

The track serpentined again, and walking ahead was Easter. Geneva and Etoile were playing at her side, edging each other out of her shadow, but when they saw who was coming up behind them, they turned and ran tearing back towards camp, running at angles, like pullets, leaving a cloud of dust as they passed by.

"Wouldn't you know!" said Jinny Love.

Easter was going unconcernedly on, her dress stained green behind; she ate something out of her hand as she went.

"We'll soon catch up—don't hurry."

The reason orphans were the way they were lay first in nobody's watching them, Nina thought, for she felt obscurely like a trespasser. They, they were not answerable. Even on being watched, Easter remained not answerable to a soul on earth. Nobody cared! And so, in this beatific state, something came out of *her*.

"Where are you going?"

"Can we go with you, Easter?"

Easter, her lips stained with blackberries, replied, "It ain't my road."

They walked along, one on each side of her. Though they automatically stuck their tongues out at her, they ran their arms around her waist. She tolerated the closeness for a little while; she smelled of orphan-starch, but she had a strange pure smell of sweat, like a sleeping baby, and in her temple, so close then to their eyes, the skin was transparent enough for a little vein to be seen pounding under it. She seemed very tender and very small in the waist to be trudging along so doggedly, when they had her like that.

Vines, a magnificent and steamy green, covered more and more of the trees, played over them like fountains. There were stretches of water below them, blue-black, netted over with half-closed waterlilies. The horizontal limbs of cypresses grew a short, pale green scruff like bird feathers.

They came to a tiny farm down here, the last one possible before the muck sucked it in—a patch of cotton in flower, a house whitewashed in front, a cleanswept yard with a little iron pump standing in the middle of it like a black rooster. These were white people—an old woman in a sunbonnet came out of the house with a galvanized bucket, and pumped it full in the dooryard. That was an excuse to see people go by.

Easter, easing out of the others' clasp, lifted her arm halfway and, turning for an instant, gave two waves of the hand. But the old woman was prouder than she.

Jinny Love said, "How would you all like to live there?"

Cat edged the woods onward, and at moments vanished into a tunnel in the briars. Emerging from other tunnels, he—or she—glanced up at them with a face more masklike than ever.

"There's a short-cut to the lake." Easter, breaking and darting ahead, suddenly went down on her knees and slid under a certain place in the barbed wire fence. Rising, she took a step inward, sinking down as she went. Nina untwined her arm from Jinny Love's and went after her.

"I might have known you'd want us to go through a barbed wire fence." Jinny Love sat down where she was, on the side of the ditch, just as she would take her seat on a needlepoint stool. She jumped up once, and sat back. "Fools, fools!" she called. "Now I think you've made me turn my ankle. Even if I wanted to track through the mud, I couldn't!"

Nina and Easter, dipping under a second, unexpected fence, went on, swaying and feeling their feet pulled down, reaching to the trees. Jinny Love was left behind in the heartless way people and incidents alike are thrown off in the course of a dream, like the gratuitous flowers scattered from a float—rather in celebration. The swamp was now all-enveloping, dark and at the same time vivid, alarming—it was like being inside the chest of something that breathed and might turn over.

Then there was Moon Lake, a different aspect altogether. Easter climbed the slight rise ahead and reached the pink, grassy rim and the innocent open. Here it was quiet, until, fatefully, there was one soft splash.

"You see the snake drop off in the water?" asked Easter.

"Snake?"

"Out of that tree."

"You can have him."

"There he is: coming up!" Easter pointed.

"That's probably a different one," Nina objected in the voice of Jinny Love.

110

Easter looked both ways, chose, and walked on the pink sandy rim with its purpled lip, her blue shadow lolling over it. She went around a bend, and straight to an old gray boat. Did she know it would be there? It was in some reeds, looking mysterious to come upon and yet in place, as an old boat will. Easter stepped into it and hopped to the far seat that was over the water, and dropping to it lay back with her toes hooked up. She looked falling over backwards. One arm lifted, curved over her head, and hung till her finger touched the water.

The shadows of the willow leaves moved gently on the sand, deep blue and narrow, long crescents. The water was quiet, the color of pewter, marked with purple stobs, although where the sun shone right on it the lake seemed to be in violent agitation, almost boiling. Surely a little chip would turn around and around in it. Nina dropped down on the flecked sandbar. She fluttered her eyelids, half closed them, and the world looked struck by moonlight.

"Here I come," came Jinny Love's voice. It hadn't been long. She came twitching over their tracks along the sandbar, her long soft hair blowing up like a skirt in a play of the breeze in the open. "But I don't choose to sit myself in a leaky boat," she was calling ahead. "I choose the land."

She took her seat on the very place where Nina was writing her name. Nina moved her finger away, drawing a long arrow to a new place. The sand was coarse like beads and full of minute shells, some shaped exactly like bugles.

"Want to hear about my ankle?" Jinny Love asked. "It wasn't as bad as I thought. I must say you picked a queer place, I saw an *owl*. It smells like the school basement to me—peepee and old erasers." Then she stopped with her mouth a little open, and was quiet, as though something had been turned off inside her. Her eyes were soft, her gaze stretched to Easter, to the boat, the lake—her long oval face went vacant.

111

"Why aren't we out in the boat?" Nina, taking a strange and heady initiative, rose to her feet. *"Out there!"*

Easter was lying rocked in the gentle motion of the boat, her head turned on its cheek. She had not said hello to Jinny Love anew. Did she see the drop of water clinging to her lifted finger? Did it make a rainbow? Not to Easter: her eyes were rolled back, Nina felt. Her own hand was writing in the sand. Nina, Nina, Nina. Writing, she could dream that her self might get away from her—that here in this faraway place she could tell her self, by name, to go or to stay. Jinny Love had begun building a sand castle over her foot. In the sky clouds moved no more perceptibly than grazing animals. Yet with a passing breeze, the boat gave a knock, lifted and fell. Easter sat up.

"Why aren't we out in the boat?" Nina, taking a strange and heady initiative, rose to her feet. "Out there!" A picture in her mind, as if already furnished from an eventual and appreciative distance, showed the boat floating where she pointed, far out in Moon Lake with three girls sitting in the three spaces. "We're coming, Easter!"

"Just as I make a castle. *I'm* not coming," said Jinny Love. "Anyway, there's stobs in the lake. We'd be upset, ha ha."

"What do I care, I can swim!" Nina cried at the water's edge.

"You can just swim from the first post to the second post. And that's in front of camp, not here."

Firming her feet in the sucking, minnowy mud, Nina put her weight against the boat. Soon her legs were half hidden, the mud like some awful kiss pulled at her toes, and all over she tautened and felt the sweat start out of her body. Roots laced her feet, knotty and streaming. Under water, the boat was caught too, but Nina was determined to free it. She saw that there was muddy water in the boat too, which Easter's legs, now bright pink, were straddling. Suddenly all seemed easy.

"It's coming loose!"

At the last minute, Jinny Love, who had extracted her foot from the castle with success, hurried over and climbed to the middle seat of the boat, screaming. Easter sat up swaying with the dip of the boat;

113

the energy seemed all to have gone out of her. Her lolling head looked pale and featureless as a pear beyond the laughing face of Jinny Love. She had not said whether she wanted to go or not—yet surely she did; she had been in the boat all along, she had discovered the boat.

For a moment, with her powerful hands, Nina held the boat back. Again she thought of a pear—not the everyday gritty kind that hung on the tree in the backyard, but the fine kind sold on trains and at high prices, each pear with a paper cone wrapping it alone—beautiful, symmetrical, clean pears with thin skins, with snow-white flesh so juicy and tender that to eat one baptized the whole face, and so delicate that while you urgently ate the first half, the second half was already beginning to turn brown. To all fruits, and especially to those fine pears, something happened—the process was so swift, you were never in time for them. It's not the flowers that are fleeting, Nina thought, it's the fruits—it's the time when things are ready that they don't stay. She even went through the rhyme, "Pear tree by the garden gate, How much longer must I wait?"—thinking it was the pears that asked it, not the picker.

Then she climbed in herself, and they were rocking out sideways on the water.

"Now what?" said Jinny Love.

"This is all right for me," said Nina.

"Without oars?—Ha ha."

"Why didn't you tell me, then!—But I don't care now."

"You never are as smart as you think."

"Wait till you find out where we get to."

"I guess you know Easter can't swim. She won't even touch water with her foot."

"What do you think a *boat's* for?"

But a soft tug had already stopped their drifting. Nina with a dark frown turned and looked down.

114

"A chain! An old mean chain!"

"That's how smart you are."

Nina pulled the boat in again—of course nobody helped her!—burning her hands on the chain, and kneeling outward tried to free the other end. She could see now through the reeds that it was wound around and around an old stump, which had almost grown over it in places. The boat had been chained to the bank since maybe last summer.

"No use hitting it," said Jinny Love.

A dragonfly flew about their heads. Easter only waited in her end of the boat, not seeming to care about the disappointment either. If this was their ship, she was their figurehead, turned on its back, sky-facing. She wouldn't be their passenger.

"You thought we'd all be out in the middle of Moon Lake by now, didn't you?" Jinny Love said, from her lady's seat. "Well, look where we are."

"Oh, Easter! Easter! I wish you still had your knife!"

"—But let's don't go back yet," Jinny Love said on shore. "I don't think they've missed me." She started a sand castle over her other foot.

"You make me sick," said Easter suddenly.

"Nina, let's pretend Easter's not with us."

"But that's what *she* was pretending."

Nina dug into the sand with a little stick, printing "Nina" and then "Easter."

Jinny Love seemed stunned, she let sand run out of both fists. "But how could you ever know what Easter was pretending?"

Easter's hand came down and wiped her name clean; she also wiped out "Nina." She took the stick out of Nina's hand and with a formal gesture, as if she would otherwise seem to reveal too much, wrote for herself. In clear, high-waisted letters the word "Esther" cut into the sand. Then she jumped up.

115

"Who's that?" Nina asked.

Easter laid her thumb between her breasts, and walked about.

"Why, I call that 'Esther.'"

"Call it 'Esther' if you want to. I call it 'Easter.'"

"Well, sit down. . . ."

"And I named myself."

"How could you? Who let you?"

"I let myself name myself."

"Easter, I believe you," said Nina. "But I just want you to spell it right. Look—E-A-S—"

"I should worry, I should cry."

Jinny Love leaned her chin on the roof of her castle to say, "I was named for my maternal grandmother, so my name's Jinny Love. It couldn't be anything else. Or anything better. You see? Easter's just not a real name. It doesn't matter how she spells it, Nina, nobody ever had it. Not around here." She rested on her chin.

"I have it."

"Just see how it looks spelled right." Nina lifted the stick from Easter's fingers and began to print, but had to throw herself bodily over the name to keep Easter from it. "Spell it right and it's real!" she cried.

"But right or wrong, it's tacky," said Jinny Love. "You can't get me mad over it. All I can concentrate on out here is missing the figs at home."

"'Easter' is real beautiful!" Nina said distractedly. She suddenly threw the stick into the lake, before Easter could grab it, and it trotted up and down in a crucible of sun-filled water. "I thought it was the day you were found on a doorstep," she said sullenly—even distrustfully.

Easter sat down at last and with slow, careful movements of her palms rubbed down the old bites on her legs. Her crest of hair dipped downward and she rocked a little, up and down, side to side, in a rhythm. Easter never did intend to explain anything unless she had to—or to force your explanations. She just had hopes. She hoped never to be sorry. Or did she?

"I haven't got no father. I never had, he ran away. I've got a mother. When I could walk, then my mother took me by the hand and turned me in, and I remember it. I'm going to be a singer."

It was Jinny Love, starting to clear her throat, who released Nina. It was Jinny Love, escaping, burrowing her finger into her castle, who was now kind, pretending Easter had never spoken. Nina banged Jinny Love on the head with her fist. How good and hot her hair was! Like hot glass. She broke the castle from her tender foot. She wondered if Jinny Love's head would break. Not at all. You couldn't learn anything through the head.

"Ha, ha, ha!" yelled Jinny Love, hitting back.

They were fighting and hitting for a moment. Then they lay quiet, tilted together against the crumbled hill of sand, stretched out and looking at the sky where now a white tower of cloud was climbing.

Someone moved; Easter lifted to her lips a piece of cross-vine cut back in the days of her good knife. She brought up a kitchen match from her pocket, lighted up, and smoked.

They sat up and gazed at her.

"If you count much on being a singer, that's not a very good way to start," said Jinny Love. "Even boys, it stunts their growth."

Easter once more looked the same as asleep in the dancing shadows, except for what came out of her mouth, more mysterious, almost, than words.

"Have some?" she asked, and they accepted. But theirs went out.

Jinny Love's gaze was fastened on Easter, and she dreamed and dreamed of telling on her for smoking, while the sun, even through leaves, was burning her pale skin pink, and she looked the most beautiful of all: she felt temptation. But what she said was, "Even after all this is over, Easter, I'll always remember you."

Off in the thick of the woods came a fairy sound, followed by a tremulous silence, a holding apart of the air.

"What's that?" creid Easter sharply. Her throat quivered, the little vein in her temple jumped.

"That's Mister Loch Morrison. Didn't you know he had a horn?"

There was another fairy sound, and the pried-apart, gentle silence. The woods seemed to be moving after it, running—the world pellmell. Nina could see the boy in the distance, too, and the golden horn tilted up. A few minutes back her gaze had fled the present and this scene; now she put the horn blower into his visionary place.

"Don't blow that!" Jinny Love cried out this time, jumping to her feet and stopping up her ears, stamping on the shore of Moon Lake. "You shut up! We can hear!—Come on," she added prosaically to the other two. "It's time to go. I reckon they've worried enough." She smiled. "Here comes Cat."

Cat always caught something; something was in his—or her—mouth, a couple of little feet or claws bouncing under the lifted whiskers. Cat didn't look especially triumphant; just through with it.

They marched on away from their little boat.

IV

One clear night the campers built a fire up above the spring, cooked supper on sticks around it, and after stunts, a recitation of "How They Brought the Good News from Ghent to Aix" by Gertrude Bowles, and the ghost story about the bone, they stood up on the ridge and poured a last song into the woods—"Little Sir Echo."

The fire was put out and there was no bright point to look into, no circle. The presence of night was beside them—a beast in gossamer, with no shine of outline, only of ornament—rings, earrings. . . .

"March!" cried Mrs. Gruenwald, and stamped down the trail for them to follow. They went single file on the still-warm pine needles,

soundlessly now. Not far away there were crackings of twigs, small, re-
gretted crashes; Loch Morrison, supperless for all they knew, was wandering around by himself, sulking, alone.

Nobody needed light. The night sky was pale as a green grape,
transparent like grape flesh over each tree. Every girl saw moths—the
beautiful ones like ladies, with long legs that were wings—and the
little ones, mere bits of bark. And once against the night, just before
Little Sister Spights' eyes, making her cry out, hung suspended a
spider—a body no less mysterious than the grape of the air, different
only a little.

All around swam the fireflies. Clouds of them, trees of them, islands
of them floating, a lower order of brightness—one could even get into a
tent by mistake. The stars barely showed their places in the pale sky—
small and far from this bright world. And the world would be bright as
long as these girls held awake, and could keep their eyes from closing.
And the moon itself shone—taken for granted.

Moon Lake came in like a flood below the ridge; they trailed downward. Out there Miss Moody would sometimes go in a boat; sometimes
she had a late date from town, "Rudy" Spights or "Rudy" Loomis, and
then they could be seen drifting there after the moon was up, far out on
the smooth bright surface. ("And she lets him hug her out there," Jinny
Love had instructed them. "Like this." She had seized, of all people,
Etoile, whose name rhymed with tinfoil. "Hands off," said Etoile.)
Twice Nina had herself seen the silhouette of the canoe on the bright
water, with the figures at each end, like a dark butterfly with wings
spread open and still. Not tonight!

Tonight, it was only the helpers, fishing. But their boat must be full
of silver fish! Nina wondered if it was the slowness and near-fixity of
boats out on the water that made them so magical. Their little boat in
the reeds that day had not been far from this one's wonder, after all.
The turning of water and sky, of the moon, or the sun, always pro-

119

Every girl saw moths—the beautiful ones like ladies, with long legs that were wings—and the little ones, mere bits of bark.

ceeded, and there was this magical hesitation in their midst, of a boat. And in the boat, it was not so much that they drifted, as that in the presence of a boat the world drifted, forgot. The dreamed-about changed places with the dreamer.

Home from the wild moonlit woods, the file of little girls wormed into the tents, which were hot as cloth pockets. The candles were lighted by Miss Moody, dateless tonight, on whose shelf in the flare of nightly revelation stood her toothbrush in the glass, her hand-painted celluloid powder box, her Honey and Almond cream, her rouge and eyebrow tweezers, and at the end of the line the bottle of Compound, containing true and false unicorn and the life root plant.

Miss Moody, with fervent frown which precluded interruption, sang in soft tremolo as she rubbed the lined-up children with "Sweet Dreams."

> *"Forgive me*
> *O please forgive me*
> *I didn't mean to make*
> *You cry!*
> *I love you and I need you—"*

They crooked and bent themselves and lifted nightgowns to her silently while she sang. Then when she faced them to her they could look into the deep tangled rats of her puffed hair and at her eyebrows which seemed fixed for ever in that elevated line of adult pleading.

> *"Do anything but don't say good-bye!"*

And automatically they almost said, "Good-bye!" Her hands rubbed and cuffed them while she sang, pulling to her girls all just alike, as if girlhood itself were an infinity, but a commodity. ("I'm ticklish," Jinny Love informed her every night.) Her look of pleading seemed infinitely perilous to them. Her voice had the sway of an aerialist crossing the high wire, even while she sang out of the nightgown coming down over her head.

There were kisses, prayers. Easter, as though she could be cold tonight, got into bed with Geneva. Geneva like a little June bug hooked onto her back. The candles were blown. Miss Moody ostentatiously went right to sleep. Jinny Love cried into her pillow for her mother, or perhaps for the figs. Just outside their tent, Citronella burned in a saucer in the weeds—Citronella, like a girl's name.

Luminous of course but hidden from them, Moon Lake streamed out in the night. By moonlight sometimes it seemed to run like a river. Beyond the cry of the frogs there were the sounds of a boat moored somewhere, of its vague, clumsy reaching at the shore, those sounds that are recognized as being made by something sightless. When did boats have eyes—once? Nothing watched that their little part of the lake stayed roped off and protected; was it there now, the rope stretched frail-like between posts that swayed in mud? That rope was to mark how far the girls could swim. Beyond lay the deep part, some bottomless parts, said Moody. Here and there was the quicksand that stirred your footprint and kissed your heel. All snakes, harmless and harmful, were freely playing now; they put a trailing, moony division between weed and weed—bright, turning, bright and turning.

Nina still lay dreamily, or she had waked in the night. She heard Gertrude Bowles gasp in a dream, beginning to get her stomach ache, and Etoile begin, slowly, her snore. She thought: Now I can think, in between them. She could not even feel Miss Moody fretting.

The orphan! she thought exultantly. The other way to live. There were secret ways. She thought, Time's really short, I've been only thinking like the others. It's only interesting, only worthy, to try for the fiercest secrets. To slip into them all—to change. To change for a moment into Gertrude, into Mrs. Gruenwald, into Twosie—into a boy. To *have been* an orphan.

Nina sat up on the cot and stared passionately before her at the night—the pale dark roaring night with its secret step, the Indian night. She felt the forehead, the beaded stars, look in thoughtfully at her.

The pondering night stood rude at the tent door, the opening fold would let it stoop in—it, him—he had risen up inside. Long-armed, or long-winged, he stood in the center there where the pole went up. Nina lay back, drawn quietly from him. But the night knew about Easter. All about her. Geneva had pushed her to the very edge of the cot. Easter's hand hung down, opened outward. Come here, night, Easter might say, tender to a giant, to such a dark thing. And the night, obedient and graceful, would kneel to her. Easter's callused hand hung open there to the night that had got wholly into the tent.

Nina let her own arm stretch forward opposite Easter's. Her hand too opened, of itself. She lay there a long time motionless, under the night's gaze, its black cheek, looking immovably at her hand, the only part of her now which was not asleep. Its gesture was like Easter's, but Easter's hand slept and her own hand knew—shrank and knew, yet offered still.

"Instead . . . me instead . . ."

In the cup of her hand, in her filling skin, in the fingers' bursting weight and stillness, Nina felt it: compassion and a kind of competing that were all one, a single ecstasy, a single longing. For the night was not impartial. No, the night loved some more than others, served some more than others. Nina's hand lay open there for a long time, as if its fingers would be its eyes. Then it too slept. She dreamed her hand was helpless to the tearing teeth of wild beasts. At reveille she woke up lying on it. She could not move it. She hit it and bit it until like a cluster of bees it stung back and came to life.

Nina sat up on the cot and stared passionately before her
at the night—the pale dark roaring night with its secret step,
the Indian night.

V

They had seen, without any idea of what he would do—and yet it was just like him—little old Exum toiling up the rough barky ladder and dreaming it up, clinging there monkeylike among the leaves, all eyes and wrinkled forehead.

Exum was apart too, boy and colored to boot; he constantly moved along an even further fringe of the landscape than Loch, wearing the man's stiff straw hat brilliant as a snowflake. They would see Exum in the hat bobbing along the rim of the swamp like a fisherman's cork, elevated just a bit by the miasma and illusion of the landscape he moved in. It was Exum persistent as a little bug, inching along the foot of the swamp wall, carrying around a fishing cane and minnow can, fishing around the bend from their side of the lake, catching all kinds of things. Things, things. He claimed all he caught, gloating—dangled it and loved it, clasped it with suspicious glee—wouldn't a soul dispute him that? The Boy Scout asked him if he could catch an electric eel and Exum promised it readily—a gift; the challenge was a siesta-long back-and-forth across the water.

Now all rolling eyes, he hung on the ladder, too little to count as looking—too everything-he-was to count as anything.

Beyond him on the diving-board, Easter was standing—high above the others at their swimming lesson. She was motionless, barefooted, and tall with her outgrown, printed dress on her and the sky under her. She had not answered when they called things up to her. They splashed noisily under her callused, coral-colored foot that hung over.

"How are you going to get down, Easter!" shouted Gertrude Bowles.

Miss Moody smiled understandingly up at Easter. How far, in the water, could Miss Parnell Moody be transformed from a schoolteacher? They had wondered. She wore a canary yellow bathing cap lumpy over her hair, with a rubber butterfly on the front. She wore a brassiere and bloomers under her bathing suit because, said Jinny Love, that was exactly how good she was. She scarcely looked for trouble, immediate trouble—though this was the last day at Moon Lake.

Exum's little wilted black fingers struck at his lips as if playing a tune on them. He put out a foolishly long arm. He held a green willow switch. Later they every one said they saw him—but too late. He gave Easter's heel the tenderest, obscurest little brush, with something of nigger persuasion about it.

She dropped like one hit in the head by a stone from a sling. In their retrospect, her body, never turning, seemed to languish upright for a moment, then descend. It went to meet and was received by blue air. It dropped as if handed down all the way and was let into the brown water almost on Miss Moody's crown, and went out of sight at once. There was something so positive about its disappearance that only the instinct of caution made them give it a moment to come up again; it didn't come up. Then Exum let loose a girlish howl and clung to the ladder as though a fire had been lighted under it.

Nobody called for Loch Morrison. On shore, he studiously hung his bugle on the tree. He was enormously barefooted. He took a frog dive and when he went through the air they noticed that the powdered-on dirt gave him lavender soles. Now he swam destructively into the water, cut through the girls, and began to hunt Easter where all the fingers began to point.

They cried while he hunted, their chins dropping into the brown buggy stuff and their mouths sometimes swallowing it. He didn't give a glance their way. He stayed under as though the lake came down a lid on him, at each dive. Sometimes, open-mouthed, he appeared with something awful in his hands, showing not them, but the world, or himself—long ribbons of green and terrible stuff, shapeless black matter, nobody's shoe. Then he would up-end and go down, hunting her again. Each dive was a call on Exum to scream again.

"Shut up! Get out of the way! You stir up the lake!" Loch Morrison yelled once—blaming them. They looked at one another and after one loud cry all stopped crying. Standing in the brown that cut them off where they waited, ankle-deep, waist-deep, knee-deep, chin-deep, they made a little V, with Miss Moody in front and partly obscuring their vision with her jerky butterfly cap. They felt his insult. They stood so still as to be almost carried away, in the pictureless warm body of lake around them, until they felt the weight of the currentless water pulling anyhow. Their shadows only, like the curled back edges of a split drum, showed where they each protruded out of Moon Lake.

Up above, Exum howled, and further up, some fulsome, vague clouds with uneasy hearts blew peony-like. Exum howled up, down, and all around. He brought Elberta, mad, from the cook tent, and surely Mrs. Gruenwald was dead to the world—asleep or reading—or she would be coming too, by now, capering down her favorite trail. It was Jinny Love, they realized, who had capered down, and now stood strangely signaling from shore. The painstaking work of Miss Moody, white bandages covered her arms and legs; poison ivy had appeared that morning. Like Easter, Jinny Love had no intention of going in the lake.

"Ahhhhh!" everybody said, long and drawn out, just as he found her.

Of course he found her, there was her arm sliding through his hand. They saw him snatch the hair of Easter's head, the way a boy will snatch anything he wants, as if he won't have invisible opponents snatching first. Under the water he joined himself to her. He spouted, and with engine-like jerks brought her in.

There came Mrs. Gruenwald. With something like a skip, she came to a stop on the bank and waved her hands. Her middy blouse flew up, showing her loosened corset. It was red. They treasured that up. But her voice was pre-emptory.

"This minute! Out of the lake! Out of the lake, out-out! Parnell! Discipline! March them out."

"One's drowned!" shrieked poor Miss Moody.

He put out a foolishly long arm. He held a green willow switch.

Loch stood over Easter. He sat her up, folding, on the shore, wheeled her arm over, and by that dragged her clear of the water before he dropped her, a wrapped bundle in the glare. He shook himself in the sun like a dog, blew his nose, spat, and shook his ears, all in a kind of leisurely trance that kept Mrs. Gruenwald off—as though he had no notion that he was interrupting things at all. Exum could now be heard shrieking for Miss Marybelle Steptoe, the lady who had had the camp last year and was now married and living in the Delta.

Miss Moody and all her girls now came out of the lake. Tardy, droop-ing, their hair heavy-wet and their rubber shoes making wincing sounds, they edged the shore.

Loch returned to Easter, spread her out, and then they could all get at her, but they watched the water lake in her lap. The sun like a weight fell on them. Miss Moody wildly ran and caught up Easter's ankle and pushed on her, like a lady with a wheelbarrow. The Boy Scout looped Easter's arms like sashes on top of her and took up his end, the shoulders. They carried her, looking for shade. One arm fell, touching ground. Jinny Love, in the dazzling bandages, ran up and scooped Easter's arm in both of hers. They proceeded, zigzag, Jinny Love turning her head toward the rest of them, running low, bearing the arm.

They put her down in the only shade on earth, after all, the table under the tree. It was where they ate. The table was itself still mostly tree, as the ladder and diving board were half tree too; a camp table had to be round and barky on the underside, and odorous of having been chopped down. They knew that splintery surface, and the ants that crawled on it. Mrs. Gruenwald, with her strong cheeks, blew on the table, but she might have put a cloth down. She stood between table and girls; her tennis shoes, like lesser corsets, tied her feet solid there; and they did not go any closer, but only to where they could see.

"I got her, please ma'am."

In the water, the life saver's face had held his whole impatience; now it was washed pure, blank. He pulled Easter his way, away from Miss Moody—who, however, had got Easter's sash ends wrung out—and then, with a turn, hid her from Mrs. Gruenwald. Holding her folded up to him, he got her clear, and the next moment, with a spread of his hand, had her lying there before him on the table top.

They were silent. Easter lay in a mold of wetness from Moon Lake, on her side; sharp as a flatiron her hipbone pointed up. She was arm to arm and leg to leg in a long fold, wrong-colored and pressed together as unopen leaves are. Her breasts, too, faced together. Out of the water Easter's hair was darkened, and lay over her face in long fern shapes. Miss Moody laid it back.

"You can tell she's not breathing," said Jinny Love.

Easter's nostrils were pinched-looking like an old country woman's. Her side fell slack as a dead rabbit's in the woods, with the flowers of her orphan dress all running together in some antic of their own, some belated mix-up of the event. The Boy Scout had only let her go to leap onto the table with her. He stood over her, put his hands on her, and rolled her over; they heard the distant-like knock of her forehead on the solid table, and the knocking of her hip and knee.

Exum was heard being whipped in the willow clump; then they remembered Elberta was his mother. "You little black son-a-bitch!" they heard her yelling, and he howled through the woods.

Astride Easter the Boy Scout lifted her up between his legs and dropped her. He did it again, and she fell on one arm. He nodded—not to them.

There was a sigh, a Morgana sigh, not an orphans'. The orphans did not press forward, or claim to own or protect Easter any more. They did nothing except mill a little, and yet their group was delicately changed.

131

He took a frog dive and when he went through the air they noticed
that the powdered-on dirt gave him lavender soles.

In Nina's head, where the world was still partly leisurely, came a recollected scene: birds on a roof under a cherry tree; they were drunk.

The Boy Scout, nodding, took Easter's hair and turned her head. He left her face looking at them. Her eyes were neither open nor altogether shut but as if her ears heard a great noise, back from the time she fell; the whites showed under the lids pale and slick as watermelon seeds. Her lips were parted to the same degree, her teeth could be seen smeared with black mud.

The Boy Scout reached in and gouged out her mouth with his hand, an unbelievable act. She did not alter. He lifted up, screwed his toes, and with a groan of his own fell upon her and drove up and down upon her, into her, gouging the heels of his hands into her ribs again and again. She did not alter except that she let a thin stream of water out of her mouth, a dark stain down the fixed cheek. The children drew together. Life-saving was much worse than they had dreamed. Worse still was the carelessness of Easter's body.

Jinny Love volunteered once more. She would wave a towel over things to drive the mosquitoes, at least, away. She chose a white towel. Her unspotted arms lifted and criss-crossed. She faced them now; her expression quietened and became ceremonious.

Easter's body lay up on the table to receive anything that was done to it. If *he* was brutal, her self, her body, the withheld life, was brutal too. While the Boy Scout as if he rode a runaway horse clung momently to her and arched himself off her back, dug his knees and fists into her and was flung back careening by his own tactics, she lay there.

Let him try and try!

The next thing Nina knew was a scent of home, an adult's thumb in her shoulder, and a cry, "Now what?" Miss Lizzie Stark pushed in front of her, where her hips and black purse swung to a full stop, blotting out

133

everything. She was Jinny Love's mother and had arrived on her daily visit to see how the camp was running.

They never heard the electric car coming, but usually they saw it, watched for it in the landscape, as out of place as a piano rocking over the holes and taking the bumps, making a high wall of dust.

Nobody dared tell Miss Lizzie; only Loch Morrison's grunts could be heard.

"Some orphan get too much of it?" Then she said more loudly, "But what's *he* doing to her? Stop that."

The Morgana girls all ran to her and clung to her skirt.

"Get off me," she said. "Now look here, everybody. I've got a weak heart. You all know that.—Is that *Jinny Love?*"

"Leave me alone, Mama," said Jinny Love, waving the towel.

Miss Lizzie, whose hands were on Nina's shoulders, shook Nina. "Jinny Love Stark, come here to me, Loch Morrison, get off that table and shame on you."

Miss Moody was the one brought to tears. She walked up to Miss Lizzie holding a towel in front of her breast and weeping. "He's our life saver, Miss Lizzie. Remember? Our Boy Scout. Oh, mercy, I'm thankful you've come, he's been doing that a long time. Stand in the shade, Miss Lizzie."

"Boy Scout? Why, he ought to be—he ought to be—I can't stand it, Parnell Moody."

"Can't any of us help it, Miss Lizzie. Can't any of us. It's what he came for." She wept.

"That's Easter," Geneva said. "That is."

"He ought to be put out of business," Miss Lizzie Stark said. She stood in the center of them all, squeezing Nina uncomfortably for Jinny Love, who flouted her up in front, and Nina could look up at her. The white rice powder which she used on the very front of her face twinkled on her faint mustache. She smelled of red pepper and lemon juice—

"Some orphan got too much of it?" Then she said more loudly, "But what's he doing to her? Stop that!"

she had been making them some mayonnaise. She was valiantly trying to make up for all the Boy Scout was doing by what she was thinking of him: that he was odious. Miss Lizzie's carelessly flung word to him on sight—the first day—had been, "You little rascal, I bet you run down and pollute the spring, don't you?" "Nome," the Boy Scout had said, showing the first evidence of his gloom.

"Tears won't help, Parnell," Miss Lizzie said. "Though some don't know what tears are." She glanced at Mrs. Gruenwald, who glanced back from another level; she had brought herself out a chair. "And our last afternoon. I'd thought we'd have a treat."

They looked around as here came Marvin, Miss Lizzie's yard boy, holding two watermelons like a mother with twins. He came toward the table and just stood there.

"Marvin. You can put those melons down, don't you see the table's got somebody on it?" Miss Lizzie said. "Put 'em down and wait."

Her presence made this whole happening seem more in the nature of things. They were glad Miss Lizzie had come! It was somehow for this that they had given those yells for Miss Lizzie as Camp Mother. Under her gaze the Boy Scout's actions seemed to lose a good deal of significance. He was reduced almost to a nuisance—a mosquito, with a mosquito's proboscis. "Get him off her," Miss Lizzie repeated, in her rich and yet careless, almost humorous voice, knowing it was no good. "Ah, get him off her." She stood hugging the other little girls, several of them, warmly. Her gaze only hardened on Jinny Love; they hugged her all the more.

She loved them. It seemed the harder it was to get out here and the harder a time she found them having, the better she appreciated them. They remembered now—while the Boy Scout still drove up and down on Easter's muddy back—how they were always getting ready for Miss Lizzie; the tents even now were straight and the ground picked up and raked for her, and the tea for supper was already made and sitting in a

tub in the lake; and sure enough, the Negroes' dog had barked at the
car just as always, and now here she was. She could have stopped
everything; and she hadn't stopped it. Even her opening protests seemed
now like part of things—what she was supposed to say. Several of the
little girls looked up at Miss Lizzie instead of at what was on the table.
Her powdered lips flickered, her eyelids hooded her gaze, but she was
there.

On the table, the Boy Scout spat, and took a fresh appraisal of
Easter. He reached for a hold on her hair and pulled her head back. No
longer were her lips faintly parted—her mouth was open. It gaped. So
did his. He dropped her, the head with its suddenness bowed again on
its cheek, and he started again.

"Easter's dead! Easter's d—" cried Gertrude Bowles in a rowdy
voice, and she was slapped rowdily across the mouth to cut off the
word, by Miss Lizzie's hand.

Jinny Love, with a persistence they had not dreamed of, deployed
the towel. Could it be owing to Jinny Love's always being on the right
side that Easter musn't dare die and bring all this to a stop? Nina
thought, It's I that's thinking. Easter's not thinking at all. And while
not thinking, she is not dead, but unconscious, which is even harder to
be. Easter had come among them and had held herself untouchable
and intact. Of course, for one little touch could smirch her, make her
fall so far, so deep.—Except that by that time they were all saying the
nigger deliberately poked her off in the water, meant her to drown.

"Don't touch her," they said tenderly to one another.

"Give up! Give up! Give up!" screamed Miss Moody—she who had
rubbed them all the same, as if she rubbed chickens for the frying pan.
Miss Lizzie without hesitation slapped her too.

"Don't touch her."

For they were crowding closer to the table all the time.

"If Easter's dead, I get her coat for winter, all right," said Geneva.
"Hush, orphan."
"Is she then?"
"You shut up." The Boy Scout looked around and panted at Geneva.
"You can ast *me* when I ast you to ast me."

The dog was barking again. Other dogs barked back.
"Now who?"
"A big boy. It's old Ran MacLain and he's coming."
"He would."
He came right up, wearing a cap.
"Get away from me, Ran MacLain," Miss Lizzie called toward him.
"You and dogs and guns, keep away. We've already got all we can put up with out here."

She put her foot down on his asking any questions, getting up on the table, or leaving, now that he'd come. Under his cap bill, Ran MacLain set his gaze—he was twenty-three, his seasoned gaze—on Loch and Easter on the table. He could not be prevented from considering them all. He moved under the tree. He held his gun under his arm. He let two dogs run loose, and almost imperceptibly, he chewed gum. Only Miss Moody did not move away from him.

And pressing closer to the table, Nina almost walked into Easter's arm flung out over the edge. The arm was turned at the elbow so that the hand opened upward. It held there the same as it had held when the night came in and stood in the tent, when it had come to Easter and not to Nina. It was the one hand, and it seemed the one moment.

"Don't touch her."

Nina fainted. She woke up to the cut-onion odor of Elberta's underarm. She was up on the table with Easter, foot to head. There was so much she loved at home, but there was only time to remember the front yard. The silver, sweet-smelling paths strewed themselves behind the

138

lawn mower, the four-o'clocks blazed. Then Elberta raised her up, she got down from the table, and was back with the others.

"Keep away. Keep away, I told you you better keep away. Leave me alone," Loch Morrison was saying with short breaths. "I dove for her, didn't I?"

They hated him, Nina most of all. Almost, they hated Easter.

They looked at Easter's mouth and at the eyes where they were contemplating without sense the back side of the light. Though she had bullied and repulsed them earlier, they began to speculate in another kind of allurement: was there danger that Easter, turned in on herself, might call out to them after all, from the other, worse, side of it? Her secret voice, if soundless then possibly visible, might work out of her terrible mouth like a vine, preening and sprung with flowers. Or a snake would come out.

The Boy Scout crushed in her body and blood came out of her mouth. For them all, it was like being spoken to.

"Nina, you! Come stand right here in my skirt," Miss Lizzie called. Nina went and stood under the big bosom that started down, at the neck of her dress, like a big cloven white hide.

Jinny Love was catching her mother's eye. Of course she had stolen brief rests, but now her white arms lifted the white towel and whipped it bravely. She looked at them until she caught their eye—as if in the end the party was for *her*.

Marvin had gone back to the car and brought two more melons, which he stood holding.

"Marvin. We aren't ready for our watermelon. I told you."

"Oh, Ran. How could you? Oh, Ran."

That was Miss Moody in still a third manifestation.

By now the Boy Scout seemed for ever part of Easter and she part of him, he in motion on the up-and-down and she stretched across. He

139

was dripping, while her skirt dried on the table; so in a manner they had changed places too. Was time moving? Endlessly, Ran MacLain's dogs frisked and played, with the Negroes' dog between.

Time was moving because in the beginning Easter's face—the curve of her brow, the soft upper lip and the milky eyes—partook of the swoon of her fall—the almost forgotten fall that bathed her so purely in blue for that long moment. The face was set now, and ugly with that rainy color of seedling petunias, the kind nobody wants. Her mouth surely by now had been open long enough, as long as any gape, bite, cry, hunger, satisfaction lasts, any one person's grief, or even protest.

Not all the children watched, and their heads all were beginning to hang, to nod. Everybody had forgotten about crying. Nina had spotted three little shells in the sand she wanted to pick up when she could. And suddenly this seemed to her one of those moments out of the future, just as she had found one small brief one out of the past; this was far, far ahead of her—picking up the shells, one, another, another, without time moving any more, and Easter abandoned on a little edifice, beyond dying and beyond being remembered about.

"I'm so tired!" Gertrude Bowles said. "And hot. Ain't you tired of Easter, laying up there on that table?"

"My arms are about to break, you all," and Jinny Love stood and hugged them to her.

"I'm so tired of Easter," Gertrude said.

"Wish she'd go ahead and die and get it over with," said Little Sister Spights, who had been thumb-sucking all afternoon without a reprimand.

"I give up," said Jinny Love.

Miss Lizzie beckoned, and she came. "I and Nina and Easter all went out in the woods, and I was the only one that came back with poison ivy," she said, kissing her mother.

140

Miss Lizzie sank her fingers critically into the arms of the girls at her skirt. They all rose on tiptoe. Was Easter dead then?

Looking out for an instant from precarious holds, they took in sharply for memory's sake that berated figure, the mask formed and set on the face, one hand displayed, one jealously clawed under the waist, as if a secret handful had been groveled for, the spread and spotted legs. It was a betrayed figure, the betrayal was over, it was a memory. And then as the blows, automatic now, swung down again, the figure itself gasped.

"Get back. Get back." Loch Morrison spoke between cruel, gritted teeth to them, and crouched over.

And when they got back, her toes webbed outward. Her belly arched and drew up from the board under her. She fell, but she kicked the Boy Scout.

Ridiculously, he tumbled backwards off the table. He fell almost into Miss Lizzie's skirt; she halved herself on the instant, and sat on the ground with her lap spread out before her like some magnificent hat that has just got crushed. Ran MacLain hurried politely over to pick her up, but she fought him off.

"Why don't you go home—now!" she said.

Before their eyes, Easter got to her knees, sat up, and drew her legs up to her. She rested her head on her knees and looked out at them, while she slowly pulled her ruined dress downward.

The sun was setting. They felt it directly behind them, the warmth flat as a hand. Easter leaned slightly over the table's edge, as if to gaze down at what might move, and blew her nose; she accomplished that with the aid of her finger, like people from away in the country. Then she sat looking out again; in another moment her legs dropped and hung down. The girls looked back at her, through the yellow and violet streams of dust—just now reaching them from Ran MacLain's flivver—the air coarse as sacking let down from the tree branches. Easter lifted one arm and shaded her eyes, but the arm fell in her lap like a clod.

There was a sighing sound from them. For the first time they noticed there was an old basket on the table. It held their knives, forks, tin cups and plates.

"Carry me." Easter's words had no inflection. Again, "Carry me."

She held out her arms to them, stupidly.

Then Ran MacLain whistled to his dogs.

The girls ran forward all together. Mrs. Gruenwald's fists rose in the air as if she lifted—no, rather, had lowered—a curtain and she began with a bleating sound, "Pa-a-ack—"

> "—*up your troubles in your old kit bag*
> *And smile, smile, smile!*"

The Negroes were making a glorious commotion, all of them came up now, and then Exum escaped them all and ran waving away to the woods, dainty as a loosened rabbit.

"Who was he, that big boy?" Etoile was asking Jinny Love.

"Ran MacLain, slow-poke."

"What did he want?"

"He's just waiting on the camp. *They're* coming out tomorrow, hunting. I heard all he said to Miss Moody."

"Did Miss Moody *know* him?"

"Anybody knows him, and his twin brother too."

Nina, running up in the front line with the others, sighed—the sigh she gave when she turned in her examination papers at school. Then with each step she felt a defiance of her own. She screamed, "Easter!"

In that passionate instant, when they reached Easter and took her up, many feelings returned to Nina, some joining and some conflicting. At least what had happened to Easter was out in the world, like the table itself. There it remained—mystery, if only for being hard and cruel and, by something Nina felt inside her body, murderous.

Now they had Easter and carried her up to the tent, Mrs. Gruenwald still capering backwards and leading on,

"—*in your old kit bag!*
Smile, girls-instead-of-boys, that's the style!"

Miss Lizzie towered along darkly, groaning. She grabbed hold of Little Sister Spights, and said, "Can *you* brush me off!" She would be taking charge soon, but for now she asked for a place to sit down and a glass of cold water. She did not speak to Marvin yet; he was shoving the watermelons up onto the table.

Their minds could hardly capture it again, the way Easter was standing free in space, then handled and turned over by the blue air itself. Some of them looked back and saw the lake, rimmed around with its wall-within-walls of woods, into which the dark had already come. There were the water wings of Little Sister Spights, floating yet, white as a bird. "I know another Moon Lake," one girl had said yesterday. "Oh, my child, Moon Lakes are all over the world," Mrs. Gruenwald had interrupted. "I know of one in Austria. . . ." And into each fell a girl, they dared, now, to think.

The lake grew darker, then gleamed, like the water of a rimmed well. Easter was put to bed, they sat quietly on the ground outside the tent, and Miss Lizzie sipped water from Nina's cup. The sky's rising clouds lighted all over, like one spread-out blooming mimosa tree that could be seen from where the trunk itself should rise.

VI

Nina and Jinny Love, wandering down the lower path with arms entwined, saw the Boy Scout's tent. It was after the watermelon feast, and Miss Lizzie's departure. Miss Moody, in voile and tennis shoes, had a

*Nevertheless, standing there with the tent slanting over him
and his arm knobby as it reached up and his head bent a little,
he looked rather at loose ends.*

date with old "Rudy" Loomis, and Mrs. Gruenwald was trying to hold the girls with a sing before bedtime. Easter slept; Twosie watched her.

Nina and Jinny Love could hear the floating songs, farewell-like, the cheers and yells between. An owl hooted in a tree, closer by. The wind stirred.

On the other side of the tent wall the slats of the Boy Scout's legs shuttered open and shut like a fan when he moved back and forth. He had a lantern in there, or perhaps only a candle. He finished off his own shadow by opening the flap of his tent. Jinny Love and Nina halted on the path, quiet as old campers.

The Boy Scout, little old Loch Morrison, was undressing in his tent for the whole world to see. He took his time wrenching off each garment; then he threw it to the floor as hard as he would throw a ball; yet that seemed, in him, meditative.

His candle—for that was all it was—jumping a little now, he stood there studying and touching his case of sunburn in a Kress mirror like theirs. He was naked and there was his little tickling thing hung on him like the last drop on the pitcher's lip. He ceased or exhausted study and came to the tent opening again and stood leaning on one raised arm, with his weight on one foot—just looking out into the night, which was clamorous.

It seemed to them he had little to do!

Hadn't he surely, just before they caught him, been pounding his chest with his fists? Bragging on himself? It seemed to them they could still hear in the beating air of night the wild tattoo of pride he must have struck off. His silly, brief, overriding little show they could well imagine there in his tent of separation in the middle of the woods, in the night. Minnowy thing that matched his candle flame, naked as he was with that, he thought he shone forth too. Didn't he?

Nevertheless, standing there with the tent slanting over him and his

145

arm knobby as it reached up and his head bent a little, he looked rather at loose ends.

"We can call like an owl," Nina suggested. But Jinny Love thought in terms of the future. "I'll tell on him, in Morgana tomorrow. He's the most conceited Boy Scout in the whole troop; and's bowlegged."

"You and I will always be old maids," she added.

Then they went up and joined the singing.

AFTERWORD

The seven short stories that make up the book *The Golden Apples*, of which "June Recital" was the first, were written during the middle or closing years of the 1940s in Jackson. All but one happen in and around an imaginary small town in the Yazoo-Mississippi Delta called Morgana—the kind that is a world to itself. The stories are connecting. They are about human relationships in their beginnings and changes among the characters in their different times, all within the frame of Morgana. The exception, "Music from Spain," happening to one Morgana character who gets himself all the way to San Francisco (it was written in San Francisco) makes its own comment on what the spell of place can do, the way it may contribute to our fates.

In writing my stories, I've always been indebted to place—most often the South. It has informed me and nourished my imagination in endless ways, but in "June Recital" I became indebted to place in a very specific respect: to an actual street location in my town.

Our family house and the Music Building of Belhaven College stood directly across the street from each other. Drifting out through the open windows of the practice rooms opposite and, floating across Pinehurst Street, in through the open windows of my upstairs room where I sat at the typewriter working, came the clear, searching, repeating sounds of piano practice. Its sound traveled unimpeded: that was a year when air conditioning had not arrived to shut us away from each other, and the traffic on our residential street hadn't yet revved up to come between us. The pupils—I never saw them once—were few in number; they

147

played in their turn, never conflicting. On their warm, young, patient or impatient fingers they practiced alone.

Though I was as constant in my work as the students were, subconsciously I must have been listening to them, following them, for some time. I realized that each practice session reached me as a solitary outpouring. And longings so expressed, so insistent, so repeated, called up still more longings *un*expressed. I began to hear, in what kept coming across the street into the room where I typed, the recurring dreams of youth, inescapable, never to be renounced, only naming themselves over and over again.

Certain pupils were working up show-pieces—the *Warsaw Concerto* as well as "Country Gardens." But it was the tender, insistent "*Für Elise*" that tugged at me, continued in my ears even when it wasn't being played; and I stopped my typing. "*Für Elise*" penetrated into my own life and found me a story to tell. It gave me "June Recital" and its perpetrator, Virgie Rainey. At the same time, another source, older, had been tapped—my memory.

Little girls when I was growing up in Jackson took piano lessons almost as a matter of course. It was inevitable (only if you were a girl, however) that you should "take"; your family was cheerfully prepared to sacrifice, if need be, so that you should not go without a piano in the home and weekly lessons from a teacher. So of course there were dozens of teachers in Jackson. None of them, as far as I knew or ever heard of, were in the least like Miss Eckhart, the other leading character in "June Recital." None of the teachers were German, to start with. And when I gave Miss Eckhart her key line, "Virgie Rainey, *danke schoen*," I had never heard German spoken. I'd only heard music-teaching spoken.

My own teacher, like most of the others, I presume, was a deep-dyed Jacksonian. Though she dipped her pen in ink and wrote "Practice!" on my sheet music with a "P" that looked like a cat with a long tail, and though she did occasionally rap my erring fingers with a fly swatter,

148

and though she had a metronome, she bore no other resemblance, inner or outer, to Miss Eckhart. She was not (so far as a child was aware) troubled by passionate feelings.

But was she a recital giver! Of course. Indeed, she was a formidable recital giver, terrifying us all through the month of June. But by the nature of their calling, all piano teachers of the young are recital givers, and all recitals are probably variations of the same anguished pattern—almost a ritual of summer—on which I freely drew for my story.

So where did Miss Eckhart, who did have passionate feelings, and who had no predecessor in my real life, come from? She was invented whole, for the purposes of "June Recital." She was not simply a teacher, she was the bringer of the entirely new dimension, that of art, to the life of Morgana, Mississippi. (And don't we all know some heroic figure like that?) She came able to perceive the natural artist in her best pupil, Virgie Rainey, to challenge her to pursue her gift, to call her to account when she rebelled, to encourage and to love her. This potent character tries and tries again, challenging, demonstrating, providing a terrifying example, suffering and demanding, on behalf of Virgie's own gift which Virgie in her carelessness and wastefulness throws away.

Miss Eckhart had, and discharged, passionate feelings. She had no real-life predecessors, and her force was unqualified, quite unsheathed, and, in its form of love, repudiated. She was one of the characters in *The Golden Apples*—perhaps the pre-emptive one—that sprang from deep within my own imagination. Perhaps all the more because she had no real-life counterpart, her force was allotted its full range. There were only children to feel that and reject it.

Both "June Recital" and "Moon Lake" are about the young. "Moon Lake" had its inception in a two-week period when for the first time in my life I was away from home without my family. I was nine years old, in a summer when groups of Jackson children went in relays across Pearl River to a camp in bosky Rankin County. It was called, I think, Camp McLaurin. We lived by a lake and slept in tents under the supervision of local young ladies attached, if I'm not now mistaken, to the Jackson Y.W.C.A. They wore middy blouses and put up their hair in puffs over the ears. One wore an Indian head-band, one played a ukelele, and they all smelled of citronella.

I finally learned how to drink water from a spring, but it just served to wring my heart with homesickness for Jackson water. Everything made me homesick, and homesickness made me tormentedly sensitive to, and startled by, everything new in the life around me. This included the fact that a matching contingent of orphans from one of the Jackson orphanages shared the two weeks with children who'd come off and left their homes and families behind, like me. They seemed to stick very close to us, but they kept mum. They didn't care to answer your first question or to ask you one back. I credited them with being homesick for their orphanage, here in the woods that smelled mockingly like Christmas trees, with red clay banks to run up and down, hot as fever to the bare feet, here by the muddy lake into which, if you looked too hard before putting your toes in, you could see the turning shadows of snakes. When we sat cross-legged around the campfire after dark and sang "There's a Long, Long Trail a-Winding into the Land of My Dreams," which we knew was a song our doughboys sang when they were "Over There," as I sang I cried. It was my only chance. After "lights out" in our tents, when we had said our prayers, we were supposed to go to sleep; but it was possible to look out where the flap in the tent was pulled back. Then, like Nina in "Moon Lake," and with her fearful rapture, I saw the whole mysterious night.

At camp that summer, nothing ever really happened in real life. But in the story, what has its beginning in nameless apprehension, and then steals up through surmise, finally takes center stage: there is the shock of a happening. While all the campers stand witness, it threatens to expose for them the secrets of the world, of life and death, in spite of a ring of chaperones. Childhood, ready or not, is jolted forward into adolescence.

"Moon Lake's" characters and events rose out of the story as the story rose out of my childhood. The invention of Easter—scornful, fearless orphan Easter—and the events of her near-drowning and the gawky ritual of rescue—were the outcome. Though the real-life situation made it possible, indeed all but called for it to happen, the plot was entirely invented. The characters too were all made up toward that end, though memory helped, and every female character probably— inevitably—had parts of me.

I have to amend the claim of inventing everybody. My brother Edward was in fact a Boy Scout, who, one summer, acted as life guard and was beleaguered in a small camp for girls; but that was in a later year, in another camp, in another part of Mississippi. I brought him, along with his bugle, to "Moon Lake," where I needed Loch. Like Loch exactly, I remembered, when Edward was at a stage where he could hardly endure the presence of girls, he lived surrounded by them, more or less at their mercy. Whatever happened at that camp, he was on hand, dwelling in boredom and disgust, but, as a Boy Scout, *prepared*. For Loch at Moon Lake I didn't change Edward a bit; he was perfect as he was. But as far as he ever mentioned, he was never called on to perform artificial respiration on anybody.

Some stories bring their writer a greater surprise of joy in the doing than others, equally absorbing or demanding, manage to bring. In the writing of *The Golden Apples*, "June Recital" and "Moon Lake" were for me so blessed.

And now they have been blessed again, from a modern source. The spirited, sensitive, wonderfully congenial black and white illustrations Mildred Nungester Wolfe has made for this book have brought to the two stories a rich additional life of their own.

Eudora Welty

This volume was designed by John A. Langston.
Titles were hand lettered by Chuck Abraham.
The text was set in 13 point Linotron Bodoni by G&S Typesetters
of Austin, Texas. It was printed on Mohawk Superfine Softwhite Smooth
by Thomson-Shore, Inc., of Dexter, Michigan, and bound by
John H. Dekker & Sons of Grand Rapids, Michigan. The binding fabric
is Holliston Kingston Natural, with
Multicolor Antique boards and endpapers.